ỌLA COMES OF AGE

ỌLA COMES OF AGE

COMFORT CHISARAOKWU NWABARA, PH.D.

SECOND CRITICAL EDITION

Edited with an introduction by

ADA UZOAMAKA AZODO, PH.D.

GOLDLINE & JACOBS PUBLISHING
GLASSBORO • MILWAUKEE

GOLDLINE AND JACOBS PUBLISHING

Published in the United States
By Goldline and Jacobs Publishing Company
P. O. Box 05404
Milwaukee, WI 53205, USA
E-mail:goldlineandjacobs@gmail.com
Website: www.goldlineandjacobs.org/index.php/about-us10 Franklin Road

Ola Comes of Age was originally published in 2014
by Comfort C. Nwabara
As *OLA: The Passage of an Igbo Girl*

The Goldline and Jacobs Publishing Critical Second Edition is published
By arrangement with the Author's Estate Executors, Administrators, Assigns
in 2022

The moral rights of the Author Comfort Chisaraokwu Nwabara have been
asserted
Database right Goldline and Jacobs Publishing (maker)

Cover Art Design by:

ISBN: 978-1-938598-50-0

Printed in the United States of America
1 2 3 4 5 6 7 8 9

CONTENTS

Reviews

Ọla is a story that explores the nature of love, of family relationships in a typical traditional Igbo society. The book, adjudged to be based on the personal experience of the author, traces the unique passage of an Igbo girl called Ọla from birth to maturity. Parents, and indeed, the whole community labored to ensure their children married rightly and in the process protected societal values.

In the midst of today's frequent collapse of relationships, Comfort Nwabara appears to be yearning for the return to the good old days when divorce was tabooed much for the same reason that God abhorred it. What a powerful and compelling relationship story for everyone to read.

(First Edition Back Cover)

An extraordinary book ...

It will be read year after year,

Linking together many generations

In a chain of well-remembered

Joy and freshness

-- CHUZZY

(First Edition Publishers)

ACKNOWLEDGMENTS

We acknowledge the many sources consulted that have help us realize this second critical edition of a personal story and an ethnographical look on Igbo beliefs, values and culture. This narrative will make a unique contribution to the understanding of human lives, worldviews and literatures worldwide. As a rule of thumb, followers enrich literary traditions with continuing work they realize standing on the shoulders of giants before them. They improve on the works, thoughts, ideas and insights of their forerunners. It is our hope that this second critical edition will become a worthy literary heritage that other critics can help to improve.

We regret that Dr. Okechi Nnadozie Nwabara, MD, the good son of his parents, who ordered this work in memory of his beloved mother, is no longer with us today to appreciate the effort that has led to the transformation of her original text for the better. We are grateful to Mr. Obioha O. Nwabara, Sr. for picking up the mantle and assisting us to ensure that this work came to fruition.

We dedicate this volume to the spirit of our dear friend Dr. Okechi Nnadozie Nwabara, MD. His spirit was around us and enveloped us every step of the way, urging us on, and clearing all obstacles in our way till this project of remediation and improvement was accomplished. Ya Gazie!

ILLUSTRATIONS

**(All photographs reprinted with permission of the
Author's Estate Executors)**

Portraits of the Author as a Young Girl

Nwabara
Christian
Wedding
Photographs

Nwabara Men

L to R: Obioha, Okechi, Rev. Samuel and Enyinnaya

Portraits of the Author as an Elder

Foreword to the First Edition

In this day and age, when tradition is portrayed as unchristian and outmoded, it is refreshing to read tradition and culture presented in a form that supports and strengthens Christian ethics in a manner that is not derogatory.

This is a story of a life experience that played out from childhood but was founded on ethics and traditions of earlier generations. It is a story of relationships that were genuine and constituted the norms of society that are virtually non-existent in this generation. For example, while it was not necessary for a man to fall in love before marriage, parents of the earlier generations had the obligation to ensure that their sons and daughters married rightly, and the whole community was part of this arrangement. The result was that divorce was tabooed, much for the same reason that God abhorred it.

The book is based on personal experience, and equivalent of an autobiography. In this respect, we will be careful in asserting that our forefathers and mothers were as noble as what we have now. I believe this book will provide sufficient justification for this claim.

Professor Mba Uzoukwu
Amafor, Isingwu,
Umuahia, Abia State
Nigeria
2014

Foreword to the Second Critical Edition

This second critical edition imposed multiple tasks well beyond merely reprinting or updating the original publication. It took head-on the special task of turning the work into literature, polishing the textual language, making critical comments on variations between the original text and this second edition, as well as making extensive annotations towards the betterment of the text. The ultimate objective was to produce a new edition that most approximates to the author's original version, accompanied, of course, with a critical apparatus. The result is the textual *Ọla Comes of Age*, a very important work from literary, anthropological, ethnological, psychological, and cultural perspectives.

As copy-editor, I corrected errors of the mechanics of language expression, readjusted the text by moving whole clauses, sentences and paragraphs forwards or backwards as needed to other locations where they fitted better. Then, as bilingual-translator, I ironed out purely Igbo forms of expression where they seeped through into the text and eased them more appropriately into the English, conveying as faithfully as possible the message of the First Edition of Departure (FED) to the Second Edition of Arrival (SEA), leaving nothing out of the original text, and refraining from interpreting the author or sweeping her uncertainties and ambiguities under the carpet. André Lefevere explains this exercise in 'rewriting' the writer's text seen often in the new approaches to the teaching of literatures, due to a lot of borrowing from translation, criticism, history and anthologizing, as follows:

> Rewriting therefore exerts an enormous influence not only on the image one literature is given of another but also on the image members of a culture are given of their own and other literatures. It is the hidden motor behind literary evolution and the creation of canons and paradigms. Rewriting is simply a cultural given of our time (…). If a

work of literature is not rewritten in one way or another, it is not likely to survive its date of publication by many years or even many months (...). Translators, critics, historians, anthologizers, professors, and journalists can project positive or negative images of a text, a writer, or a literature. The power of these rewriters should be analyzed, as well as the various ways in which they tend to exercise it. If it is analyzed seriously and comprehensively, it will tell us much about the influence of power and ideology on creation and education, one of the main issues of our time.[1]

Indeed, in recreating the original text, I checked all the uncertain parts of the textual ambiguities and uncertainties, corrected mistakes of detail, fleshed out hidden ideas in unclear sentences, unearthed other ideas subsumed under compacted sentences, and explained cultural items where necessary to aid the comprehension of the *Ola Comes of Age* as a literary nonfiction. More specifically, I retitled the entire text, modified titles of the second, fifth and last chapters to align them with the narrative style of this edition. A new chapter seven, "Engagement," the crucial last stage of the entire marriage transaction before the heroine's husband claims her from her father's house for the consummation of their marriage in his own house (subsumed in chapter six in the original edition, "Betrothal,") is now a chapter of its own. Hence, there are now a total of nine chapters, as opposed to eight chapters in the first edition. Finally, I reread the text of the SEA a few more times, filling in lacunas until satisfied that the final product flowed better with each new reading.

Igbophones and all other general readers interested in studies of the Igbo people, indigenous peoples, ethnography, colonialism, marriage traditions, family, love relationships, ethnicity, minority studies, diversity studies, masculinity,

---

[1] André Lefevere, *Translating Literature: Practice and Theory in Comparative Literature Context* (New York: The Modern Language Association of America, 1992, Chapter 1, pp. 13-14).

femininity, women, gender, social justice, feminism, sexuality, (auto) biography, initiation, ritual, rite of passage, and socialization of youth, will find this book to be a significant resource. University students can get a glimpse into the pre-colonial world of indigenous Igbo people and their communal institutions. They can learn that the Igbo worldview, cosmology and spirituality favor the centrality of Chukwu or Chineke as the ultimate judge of all human beings, which fact explains his predominance in names given to children at birth. Furthermore, they can learn about the fluidity of gender among the traditional Igbo men and women, who play different roles in labor and play and exert power and influence according to the occasion as gender performers. Fourth, they can (re) examine the issue of love, relationships and romance among the Igbo in particular and traditional peoples in general in the past, present and in the future. Fifth, they also can avail themselves of the opportunity to compare notions of power and privilege vis-à-vis patriarchy. Sixth, with local vision expanded into the global realm learners can explore the idea that racism and patriarchy are two sides of the same coin, and that perhaps Atlantic Slavery and colonization have a lot in common about their structure and execution under imperialism and colonialism. What were and still are their after-effects on individuals in particular and society in general? Did imperialism delay, obstruct or destroy traditional development and evolution of indigenous peoples?

Clearly, *Ọla Comes of Age* is a significant book; it allows its readers to examine and question traditional practices with contemporary critical eyes, and measure the impact of modernity on these institutions for individuals and the collectivity now and going forward into the future.

Professor Ada Uzoamaka Azodo
Indiana University Northwest
Gary, Indiana , USA 2022

Who's Who in Ọla Comes of Age

Ọla   [short for Ọlaọcha, meaning in the English "Silver", as different from Ọlaedo, which translates as "Gold" in the English. Ọla is the infant bride bespoken before her birth to a man her senior by many years, thanks to a traditional arrangement between their families that knew each other well, respected each other and wanted to cement the social and economic relationships between their families through the marriage of their son and daughter.

Name "Silver" is a precious metal of great worth. Ọla, as her mother's first-born child and first daughter in the narrative, *Ọla Comes of Age*, has the primary responsibility of helping her mother in doing her domestic chores, while learning to be a woman (wife and mother) in her culture.

Ama   (Amamba is the son of Igwe of Ajala village, the favored suitor that later married Ọla.

Igwe   Amamba's father is Elder and Head of his large family compound in Ajala village.

Agụ   One of Ọla's mother's many suitors and her favorite, became the middleman for the marriage of Ọla and Amamba.

Umunna   Kinsmen of the same clan and related by blood, living in the same vicinity, may not intermarry with Umuada, their female kin.

Umuada   Kinswomen related by blood and living in the
          same village with their Umunna are forbidden
          to intermarry with them. They may marry
          away into another village.

Elder   Compound Head and invariably the oldest married
         man in the clan or village.

Ani   Mother Earth, often known as The Earth Goddess

Ugo   [Ugonma; alias Agụnwanyị (Tiger Woman)] is the
         Mother of the narrative and Ọla's birth mother. First-
         born child and first daughter of her own mother, she
         had the primary responsibility of helping her mother to
         do her household chores and learned thereby to
         prepare to successfully be a woman, wife and mother in
         her culture. Ugonma's marital family later became
         polygamous, first due to her initial infertility problem,
         and later other reasons that necessitated still more
         acquisition of wives by her husband's second wife and
         then by their husband himself. She was elevated to the
         status of Senior Wife above other secondary wives, a
         manager of sorts for the entire polygamous compound.

Father   Ọla's Father, (alias 'Bekee'), meaning, 'Whiteman.' He
         acquired white men's mannerisms as a house slave, in
         service to the slave masters for many years during his
         childhood. Later, he became head of his own
         polygamous household.

Ọla's Aunt   Unnamed. Ọla's mother's sister, with her
              husband sheltered Ọla in a big city in her
              formative years, and so saved her from her
              ordeal of infant bride status for a while.

Principal   Unnamed Ọla's principal and mentor at the

Methodist Girls' Secondary School.

Ọla's Siblings in descending order of seniority

Onyekwere — First-born child, 1st son, meaning, "Whoever believed *his mother could bear a child?*"

Comfort — Second-born child, 1st daughter, meaning, "I am exonerated and comforted by God."

Chukwumaobi — Third-born child, 2nd son, meaning, "God knows the yearning of my heart and soul."

Mgbeudo — Fourth-born child, 2nd daughter, meaning, "A time of Peace"

Ebere — Fifth-born child, 3rd daughter, meaning, "God's mercy"

Introduction

ỌLA COMES OF AGE UPDATES AND reintroduces to a global reading public a seminal work on the heroine Ọla's transition from infanthood to adulthood as literature, against the ethnographical background of the values, cultural beliefs and worldviews of the Igbo people.

The Igbo village is presented as a safe environment in which everyone knows everyone else. They look out for one another with love and obedience to the set rules and guidelines of the community. This village structure expressly protects all that dwell within its boundaries. Eight market days make up one week, with a half week repeating itself every four market days: Eke, Orie, Afọ, and Nkwọ. Division of labor and economic activities revolve around binary male and female sex roles within nuclear and extended families respectively of monogamous and polygamous marriages set within a patrilineal political structuring. Festivals for relaxation and entertainment punctuate the drudgery of everyday monotonous existence, especially the New Yam Festival that marks the height and the renewal of the people's cyclical simple life in synch with the seasons and surrounding nature. The village scene of the beginning chapter all but recreates and revivifies an archetypal traditional Igbo cultural environment, complete with an account of the males and females that live there, their relationships in a kinship system of government, marriage with affine, occupations, festivities and entertainment, sanitation and hygiene, and values for survival and procreation in a harsh world.[1]

The textual literary prose style includes a large number of digressions, exclamations, apostrophes, reflections, and projections into the future dotted with journalistic jottings, letters, lists, and documents, all of which mirror admirable authorial artistry. In an individual context, Ọla's experience comes across as a test of physical courage, bravery and toughness, but also of the triumph of the human spirit. In a social context, however, Ọla's story provides a window into relationships and marriage in the past and the present. A subtitle of *Ọla Comes of Age* could be "Love Relationships and Marriage in Igboland: Values, Beliefs, Customs and Worldview." This trend of logic justifies the significant ending to Ọla's story as a successful journey not only of the two married persons, but also of their two families and two villages.[2] It is a peculiar ending that posits *Ọla Comes of Age* at once as a successful initiation and the end of a veritable rite of passage. Throughout the reading, we follow the heroine as she negotiates her way through life's trials and tribulations from infanthood to her maturity in adulthood.

From the peculiar ending of the story emerges a critical patriarchal theory that legitimizes a double-standard of power sharing. Whereas men are free, for example, to be promiscuous, girls are expected to be virgins for their first marriage. As wives, they must remain resilient under abusive marriages with no access to divorce they initiate and with little or no control over their bodies. They are persecuted at the faintest suspicion of infidelity.[3] They have responsibility for the food preparation, birthing, rearing and raising the next generations of children, working from dawn to dusk only to return to the daily routine at cock's crow the next day. As females, they are expected to not only to be industrious in farming and trading, but also to do the domestic chores around the house, in order to be seen and accepted as 'good,'[4] otherwise they are branded as 'bad'. Therefore, some pertinent questions come to mind. Did love exist in traditional Igbo society? Did spouses choose one another in Igboland? Did the married man and woman have a closed relationship as a couple? Were men and women equitably dowered? How did Igbo society inculcate into the youth the meaning of marriage, its ramifications and responsibilities, purposes and rewards, and rules and guidelines? How did the traditional *Ị̀gbankwụ* ceremony[5] that formalized the state of being married compare to the colonial Church Missionary Society wedding? What roles did the father and mother play in bringing up children in the family and socializing them into the larger society? How did the mother particularly inculcate in her daughters the lessons on virtue, contraception, childbirth, nursing, teaching, training, disciplining, loving and comforting a child? Was divorce an option for unsatisfactory marriages? Were adoptions, step-parenthood or remarriage acceptable and viable options when death struck and ended a marriage?

Traditionally speaking, the community's primary concern was procreation and survival, given that it was a child-oriented society.[6] In order to avoid calamitous errors, such as childlessness,[7] should the wrong choices be made, there were set traditional criteria for evaluating a suitor or would-be bride and family. Families investigated one another thoroughly and under cover. Apart from being a healthy and living human being, a suitor had to be approved by the girl's nuclear and extended families, regarding family's size, image and resources. A girl eventually had a choice too as to the age, looks, dressing and financial resources of the young man.[8] The groom's nuclear and extended families also cared for like answers to similar questions about the girl and her background. That would explain in part why girls were often married off early in childhood and before puberty, to shield them from potential sexual promiscuity that could tarnish their image and those of their families, especially if their sexual escapades resulted in a bastard baby. When such child brides were not sent to live with the family of the suitor under the umbrella of the '*Iru-mgbede*,'[9] to learn the customs and preferences of their marital families until they were ready for marriage at menarche, they remained in their natal families learning the customs and the culture that governed their future roles as wives and mothers. Metaphorically, they walked in their mothers' footsteps as they learned. That would also explain how they were merely child brides that married before puberty and why many would-be husbands were decades older than their brides. It was believed that the older a husband was the better he could take care of his wife. From that angle of vision, *Ọla Comes of Age* is a textual indictment of infanthood and childhood betrothal arranged by parents for their own social and economic interests and ambitions. Ọla refused her betrothal in infanthood and eventually married a suitor of her own approval in a love union of two mature adults of equal status, an isogamy of sorts.

Many types of marriage prevail in Igboland. There is polygamy (plural or multiple marriages),[10] be it polygyny (marriage of one man to more than one woman) or polyandry (marriage of one woman to more than one man, or even another woman),[11] which is still a common-law custom of the Igbo people, despite the prevalence of monogamy (marriage of one man to one woman only) espoused principally by the Christians. Only the Christian Church in modern times frowns on polygyny and will charge a man of bigamy if discovered. The wealthy, the privileged and the peasantry indulged and still do indulge in multiple or plural marriages for several reasons, including childlessness, lack of male children, ego flattery, and death of a spouse. Polygyny takes place more frequently in Igboland than polyandry, for families need a lot of children, especially male children, to carry on the family name and prolong the legacy of their benefactors. Infertility, male-child preference, need for more hands to work on the family businesses, desire for more female partners to flatter the ego, lust and selfishness to have more wives with whom to sleep during the time that a wife is nursing her new-born baby are also reasons for acquiring multiple wives. Igbo polyandry is more complex, though, because women who indulge in it are sometimes those whose husbands do not satisfy sexually or financially or both, women who would clandestinely go to male relatives of their husbands in the extended family or oth-

er men outside of it to get satisfaction, and widows who remain in the homestead after the passing away of their husband
to procreate with members of the extended family that they
choose themselves or who impose themselves on them by levirate marriages. Observe that the bloodline option in cases of
widowhood prohibits copulation with strangers and forbids
incestuous liaisons. Hence, through levirate marriages, custom
requires a man to 'cover' his dead brother's family by marrying his widow and continuing to procreate in the extended
family on his behalf. In exogamy (marriage outside a social
group or class), bride price is required to be paid to the girl
and her family. By the same token, the girl and her family are
expected to bring a dowry to their in-laws' home. Even in en-
dogamy (marriage within a social group), such as the Osu in-
stitution of untouchables, bride price is required and dowry
expected. Clearly, parental involvement, or even pressure, is
imperative to get the best possible marriage scenario for their
daughters' and sons' marriages in traditional Igboland. Parents prefer hypergamy, when their daughters marry up their
family social class, not hypogamy when they marry down
their social family status.

Therefore, Igbo marriage is often said to be much more a
business deal than it is a love marriage.[12] A middleman invariably makes smooth the rough edges of the pathway and processes of marriage alliances and negotiations. Fathers exert all
their powers to get as much wealth and resources as possible
from the would-be husband of their daughter and his family.
If the bride is a virgin, pretty, charming, healthy, of good character and has a job or profession, or is already working towards one, she can get away with not putting down a substan-
tial dowry in form of money or other valuables as her
contributions to the union. Where she contributes property or
money, she has a say as to its management. Still, she is expected as a good human being to allow her husband to share
in it and have a say about how it is used. Nonetheless, dowry
or bride price is not entirely a prerequisite for marriage in Ig-

boland. It is rather a way that both sides of in-laws demon-
strate the worth and value they put on their children. Mothers
are interested in their daughters falling into good ground, so
that in times of need they can count on them for succour and
help. Therefore, mothers have a duty to present marriageable
daughters to the in-laws and the society at large, but they also
care about the quality of the in-laws. Their roles go beyond
teaching to cook and clean, for they also teach them about
cosmetics, cheerfulness and smiles and the feminine art of pre-
tence as ways of enhancing their personal charm and beauty.
A scented body powder here and a sweet-smelling lotion or
pomade there go a long way to make a given girl truly marriageable.

Above all, *Ọla Comes of Age* identifies Igbo core values and
realities of relationships and marriage well beyond the personal story of the heroine, Ọla. One cardinal lesson to learn is
that traditional marriage in Igboland did not require a love
affair between the two people to be married to happen and be
successful. Moreover, Igbo marriage was not static. It is devel-
oping and continues to do so towards a future yet unknown.
The future has not yet crystalized and could be interesting to
watch when compared with countries of Asia, Europe and
America. Igbo people are steadily on the march towards a new
future of love relationships and marriage alliances as their culture undergoes modifications and changes in a global world. It
is incomprehensible, however, that in marriage Igbo people
manage to maintain very close ties and relationships with kin
and affine, yet they cool off from the dead and fear the living-
dead when death strikes and the obsequies are over.

In creating Ọla's story Nwabara exploited fully the value
of her doctoral training in Family Ecology. A sub-discipline of
Sociology, it is an interdisciplinary and transdisciplinary field
of knowledge, which focuses on the relationships between
humans in their natural and built environments. It includes
areas of knowledge as far afield as ecology, geography, ethnography, psychology, anthropology, epidemiology, zoology,

public health, domestic science and more. In all their daily activities, including pursuit of wealth, setting of values, lifestyles, creativity, use of resources and making of waste, humans relate with one another in their environment. They do so spatially and temporally, through the social, economic and political structures they have put in place. They employ their minds to tease out the best means for survival and endurance, because they understand that the interest and survival of the group must necessarily take precedence over individual interests and ambitions and that tried and adopted values must be preserved at all costs. Towards the maintenance of peace, they set and maintain boundaries and obligations, and rules and guidelines, what is known as 'inputs.' Inputs result into 'actions' and actions give rise to 'outputs' or 'outcomes,' ranging from possessions that accrue to individuals and families to services, obligations expected from kith and kin as payments. Put differently, humans may enjoy independence and autonomy, but are also bound by obligations, boundaries and orders from the group. That is precisely the thesis that has guided the creation of *Ǫla Comes of Age* in which the author passionately affirms and defends Igbo traditional values, even as she eulogizes the environment and time in a captivating first-person narrative. The authorial double vision obligates attention to the natural and supernatural elements and the thought processes and behaviors of her Igbo people in their geographical space and time period. Noteworthy is the constant and repeated reference to the historical past in such expressions as "at that time," "in their time," "in those days…" All the human activities of the Igbo people highlighted in Ǫla's story mirror ancestral roots and the beliefs and worldviews of the Igbo as a people, turning the author's unique art of storytelling of the passage of a young girl from childhood to adulthood into a yearning for the restoration, regeneration and reintegration of Igbo traditions and epistemologies.

BIOGRAPHY: LIFE AND TIMES

Comfort Chisaraokwu Nwabara (alias Nma), Ph. D., Family Ecologist, educator and writer, taught at several levels in the United States of America and Nigeria, was Acting Dean, School of Food Science and Storage Technology, Michael Okpara University of Agriculture, Umudike, Nigeria, and traversed many valleys and mountains with great courage, power and humility to achieve her myriad life-time accomplishments.

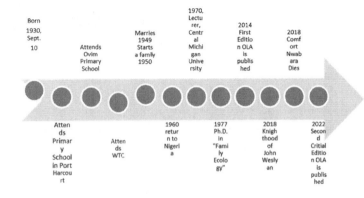

- **1930, September 10:**

Born Comfort Chisaraokwu Ọgụ, Ụmụawa, Alaọcha, Abia State, Nigeria; first daughter and second child of Pa Daniel Ọgụ and Ma Ọlaọcha Ọhaeri

Siblings in descending order of seniority are two brothers, Godwin Ọgụ Ọhaeri and Friday Ọgụ Ọhaeri; and two sisters, Felicia Ogwo and Ebere Agbara.

Attends primary school in Port-Harcourt (P.H.), living with an aunt and going back to visit her natal family only on holidays.

Attends Methodist Girls' Secondary School, Ovim, Abia State, from where she obtains her First School Leaving Certificate.

Attends Women Teachers' College (WTC), Umuahia, Abia

State, from where she obtains her Grade 2 Teacher's Certificate.

Meets Rev. Samuel Nwankwo Nwabara of the Methodist Church during her growing years
Her parents withhold permission for their marriage until she finishes her teacher's training course at the WTC and works for a year to help provide support for her family.

She then teaches at the Ndoro Primary School for one year after her graduation from WTC.

- **1949**:
Marries Rev. Samuel Nwankwo Nwabara, whom she affectionately calls SN
- **1950**:
Starts a family with husband Reverend Samuel Nwabara; lecturing at the WTC. In descending order of seniority, the children born to them are: Ada Chisaraokwu Sandra, Okechi Nnadozie, Enyinnaya Chimeremeze, Obioha Onyeije, and June Ijeoma.

- **1958**:
Travels to the United States to join her husband who had been attending the Wesleyan University, Kansas, since for his Bachelor's degree in 1956

- **1960-1961**:
Returns with husband to Nigeria from the United States and lives and works with husband at the Methodist College, Uzuakoli

- **1962-1966**:
Teaches at the University Primary School on the campus of the University of Nigeria (UNN), Nsukka, while her husband lectures at the university

- **1967-1970:**

Studies at Mount Union College, Alliance, Ohio, later transferring to Michigan State University, East Lansing, Michigan; Earns a Bachelor's degree in Home Economics and a Master's degree in Child Psychology from Michigan State University; Gains admission into the Family Ecology doctoral program, Central Michigan University (CMU), Mt. Pleasant, Michigan.

The Nigeria-Biafra war is raging and she works long hours on multiple jobs to send home scarce provisions to her husband and children. She is extremely active in raising awareness about the war, and successfully helps to raise relief aid for Biafrans suffering from blockades and attendant food shortages. Her efforts and those of other Biafrans are widely published in world media in the United States. By 1969, she successfully brings her four children to join her in Michigan, leaving behind her first son, Okechi, then a Biafran soldier, and her husband serving as Acting Internal Affairs Minister in the Biafran government headed by General Chukwuemeka Odumegwu Ojukwu.

- **1970:**

Lectures at Central Michigan University, Mt. Pleasant, Michigan, and receives a second Master's degree in Education there.

- **1977:**

Earns a Ph.D. in Family Ecology from the Michigan State University, Mt. Pleasant, Michigan

Ph.D. Thesis: "Factors Affecting Formal Education Decisions in Extended Families of the Igbo of Nigeria."

Moves back to Nigeria from the United States of America. Teaches at the Alvan Ikoku College of Education, and then later at the Abia State University is pioneer Head of the Department of Home Economics and later the Acting Dean, School of Food Science and Storage Technology, Michael Okpara University of Agriculture, Umudike in Umuahia, Abia State, Nigeria.

Pursues healthcare and education, and advocates for women in general and especially widows under the banner of Advancement for Women's Program of the First Lady of Imo State and under the umbrella of the Better Life for Rural Women's Program of the First Lady of Abia State.

Member, Church Committee, St. Stephen's Methodist Church of Nigeria, Amachara, Umuahia, Abia State, Nigeria.

Leader, Church Committee, St. Stephen's Methodist Church of Nigeria, Amachara, Umuahia, Abia State, Nigeria.

After retirement, continues to promote wellness through St. Stephen's Methodist Church, while supporting various other causes.   Founds St. Stephen's Methodist Church primary school that later adds a nursery school and a secondary school. Thanks to her lobbying efforts, that Church transforms to St. Stephen's Methodist Cathedral.

- **2018**
Knight of the Order of John Wesleyan

Member, Umuawa Daughters Meeting; the Ọkaiụga Daughters Meeting; Nneọma Council, Order of the Federal Government Council (OFG); Member, Nne-nke-Okwukwe Group of St. Stephen's Methodist Church; Order of Women (OOW) of the Methodist Church, Nigeria; Nneọma Ụmụegolu Family, Amachara; Patron, Boys and Girls Brigade, and Matron, Sunday Schools Department, Methodist Church of Nigeria (MCN), Diocese of Umuahia West.

- **1983-2018:**

Loves traveling and visits many places in her lifetime, including America, Nigeria, Israel, Jamaica, England, New Zealand and Australia.

Lives in Nigeria, but visits the United States of America often and for extended periods of time to help raise her 13 grandchildren born there and to pass on her legacy of values, wellness, hard work, honesty, self-preservation, and education.

Passionately watches Soap Operas, Jeopardy, and Wheel of Fortune; does crossword puzzles, and plays the Scrabble. Teaches her grandchildren to play checkers and enjoy American football.

A proud grandma, she is present at most of her grandchildren's graduations from their educational institutions. A great cook, she spoils the grandchildren with delicious dishes.

The grandchildren — Naomi, Olaọcha, Chisara, Chika, Nnadozie, Jasmine, Obioha, Jr., Odochi, Maxim, Okechi, Kelechi, Ụzọma, and Acha--prize her presence, coolness, steadfast demeanor, intelligence and thoughtfulness.

- **1985:**

Publishes journal article; Nwabara, C. C. "The Home Setting for Teaching and Learning." *Journal of Home Economics* (formerly *Home Echo*), Department of Home Economics, Adeyemi College of Education, Ondo: Volume 1: (June), 1985: pp. 61-68. ISSN: 01869 8345

- **1986**:

Publishes *Home Management Residency*. Owerri: Imo State Government Printer. 98 pages

- **1997**:

Reverend Samuel Nwankwo Nwabara dies

- **2014**:

Publishes *ỌLA: The Passage of an Igbo Girl*. Umuahia: Chuzzy Services Nigeria. 113 pages

- **2018**:

Comfort Chisaraokwu Nwabara, Ph.D. (née Daniel Ogu) dies

- **2022**:

 Posthumous publishing of *Ọla Comes of Age* (Second Critical Edition of *ỌLA: The Passage of an Igbo Girl*. Edited with an introduction by Dr. Ada Uzoamaka Azodo)

THE CHARACTER OF ỌLA

The authorial creation of the portrait of Ọla as protagonist, narrator, and author's persona is very important in understanding *Ọla Comes of Age*, a work based on traditional Igbo view of love relationships and marriage alliances for survival and procreation in a harsh natural and built environment.[13] Many Igbo girls of the older generations went through the ordeal of living with marriages arranged by their parents at their birth, or even before they were born, to males they had no feelings for or desire to identify with as spouses, only because their two families agreed to join them in matrimony.[14] Modernity has made it possible for these girls to courageously consider other options for living fulfilling lives, not the least of which is to openly love and predicate marriage upon romantic love. The reader can judge whether Ọla's rebellious response to her predicament is justified and whether girls who find themselves in situations of child bridehood have loopholes of escape.

Ọla is the principal character of *Ọla Comes of Age* one can consider as protagonist, narrator, and author's persona. That strategy allows us to fairly separate the text into three parts. As protagonist, Ọla matures from her days as an infant bride to a full-grown adult woman with choice as to her marriage partner. In the first three chapters of the text, chapters 1-3, then, she battles her fate of a girl engaged to be married without her consent or choice as an infant. Luckily, she escapes the sordid situation at menarche, but not without some psychological damage. In the next four chapters, chapters 4-7, she lives fairly normally, struggles with learning to be a woman in her culture, attends formal school, competes with age mates, until she finds an opportunity to perpetuate her genes with a man of her choice, marry him and start a family.[15] The last two chapters, chapter 8 and chapter 9 are on her engagement and marriage, along with bearing and rearing of children while working at her employment as a certified school teacher. Throughout the nine chapters of the book, Ọla berates traditional and loveless marriage alliances by parental arrangement, although refrains from condemning other aspects of the culture that she finds valuable. That the traditional unions manage to outlast modern ones based on romantic love do not seem to recommend them to her. Furthermore, that divorce is highly discouraged traditionally does not seem to exonerate the act of child betrothal to her. Hence, Ọla eulogizes the modern times in which spouses choose each other in a love marriage, although it comes, sadly, with a measure of promiscuity and divorce.

As narrator Ọla, juxtaposes herself and the author of the text, giving away the understanding that the narrator is also the author. The narrator, for example, perhaps inadvertently, links herself to the author when narrating the names of her siblings: "As it turned out, I was the second child and the first daughter. My parents named me *Comfort*, meaning, "*Exonerated and Comforted by God.*"[16]

In her role as narrator, she uses the first-person narrative advantageously and disadvantageously. Advantageously, she directly speaks to the reader about her experiences and the customs and mores of her Igbo people. Disadvantageously, however, the reader is limited to her views and has no other way of knowing whether she is a reliable witness and reporter. It is, however, a narrative writing style that is accessible and allows the recount in her voice incidents, odors, smells, sounds, and feelings. Ọla is able to directly render things and events exclusively from her own angle of vision. The reader, limited to her account of her personal story and her exposition of Igbo culture as she sees and knows it, learns that Ọla starts off her earthly journey as an infant bride unable to make choices about her life, fate and destiny. Later, under the tutelage of her aunt, mother and other female guides and mentors in the image of the mother--her school principal at the Methodist Girls' School, teachers, friends of her mother and other female relatives in the extended family in the village--she goes through a rebellious adolescence during which time she successfully shakes off the shackles binding her as bride to a man old enough to be her father and for whom she has no feelings or attachment. Later, she is betrothed to a suitor of her choice. After the engagement ceremony, she marries him and starts a family with him.

Finally, in full awareness of her new self-identity as a grown woman, wife and mother, she has in-depth knowledge of what is appropriate or inappropriate to do according to set adult communal standards, beliefs and worldview in her village. For example, in full possession of the existential and symbolic knowledge of the mysteries of sex, birth and death, she enjoys a marital relationship with her husband based on equality and mutuality. She makes decisions in full awareness of her rights and responsibilities to her nuclear and extended families, but also of her duties and obligations to her own life, her in-laws, her marital village and the world beyond. Having mastered her suffering and developed her unique and essential personhood in her new family, her subsequent tenacity of purpose, boldness, fearlessness, strength and endurance are worthy tenets of character for young girls all over the world to emulate. The author attests thereby to a few home truths; that the heroine's experiences teach that our humanity is indeed common and is the same for all humans; that all can come together through such phenomenal experiences as her heroine's when repeated again and again; that any stage of life comes with its own peculiar problems that can be solved and challenges that can be overcome; that by pulling together all the disparate life's experiences one can always pull through, even against all odds, and that the end eventually is all that counts.

The prior two aspects of the character of Ọla considered above as protagonist and narrator come full circle in the third aspect, Ọla as the author's persona. But, this view may severely limit, if not complicate, *Ọla Comes of Age* as literature. Is it an autobiography? Is it a biography? Is it fiction? Is it nonfiction? Given the abundance of literary techniques and devices employed in presenting factual and ethnographical information, along with the point of view of the subject matter, style and genre, this work could be characterized as creative nonfiction, literary nonfiction or narrative nonfiction. First, the subject matter is verifiable when the story-like arc is placed side by side with the author's biography. The text as a fictional invention has not been able to wholly escape the known and documented boundaries for narrative nonfiction. Indeed, the author has brought to bear some novel perspectives in relating her research on the subject matter of family, the impact of the environment on it, and the credibility of her assertions. Second, the text employs hyperbole in relating events. During the heroine's homecoming, for example, the narrator makes reference to Chinua Achebe's proverbial exaggeration in his premier novel.[17] She states: "The soup had more ingredients in it than was normally expected. And, of course, the mound of cassava fufu was high to the roof top, perhaps higher than the one Chinua Achebe so eloquently described in hyperbolic terms during an in-laws get-together in his famous premier novel, *Things Fall Part*.[18]

Ọla Comes of Age is a personal story, which in the end is an authorial exploitation of language and ethnography to relate a subjective experience. Françoise Lionnet describes such writings as works of autoethnography (the neologism is poignant), although she speaks with reference to Zora Neale Hurston's *Dust Tracks on a Road*.[19] They are indeed works so peculiar to themselves that one cannot compare them to any others that had been done before them.[20] They are self-contained texts, states Michel Beaujour, "*des textes qui se tiennent par eux-mêmes, plutôt que la mimesis d'actions passées*,"[21] texts so peculiar to themselves, that they are by no means re-presentations over again of earlier texts in the same style or genre.

ỌLA AS SPOKESPERSON

Clearly, the author employs Ọla in *Ọla Comes of Age* as her tool for making comments on the traditional customs of the Igbo people regarding love and marriage. Ọla is a good choice for this role, given her several conflicting and complex experiences in childhood until her maturity in adulthood. Her experiences include first-hand childhood as infant bride. Following her liberation from her ordeal as an infant bride and later her exposure to the missionary schools and religion, she states:

> Thus, I grew up believing that I was already married. That was a rightful assumption, for there was no way I could have changed the situation, had I even tried. Yes, indeed, everyone in the village labeled me as married, even while still living in my maternal home. That affiancing denied me my childhood and kept me on a leash. I dare any modern-day psychologist to analyze the practice of infant be-

trothal and affirm an adequate understanding of its horrendous effects on the victim's character, in this instance,
mine. Had psychologists existed at the time and dared to
carry out any such studies, they would have met strong
opposition in the village. In those days, the villagers would
have driven them out of their community.[22]

Contrarily to her disgust with the arranged marriage, later
on Ọla boldly gives full rein to her inner passion and desire.
Amamba literally swept her off her feet. She poignantly describes their meeting in the market square in a remarkable direct first-person account:

> (…) My discomfort was mounting by the minute. I could
> only manage and control myself by looking away from
> this taunting stranger, by focusing my eyes on the ground.
> (…) Thoughts of him that I would characterize as 'bad',
> continued to invade my sensibility. Those thoughts caused
> me to shiver and tremble, as I became conscious of my
> emotional vulnerabilities that hitherto were un-beknownst
> to me. I was still lost in deep thoughts of Ama to the extent
> that when mother returned and handed me my blood sau-
> sage I did not want to eat it immediately. Instead, I told her
> that I would take it home and share with my siblings.
> (…).[23]

American mythologist, writer and Professor Joseph
Campbell states that when soulmates meet their worlds are
completely changed. They know and recognize each other and
they are no longer the persons they used to be after that.[24] Ọla
and Amamba knew and recognized each other and their lives
changed, forever.

Noteworthy is Ọla's mixed emotions about her culture vis-à-
vis love relationships and marriage. Employing the literary
device of apostrophe, she interprets her narrative after render-
ing it, and directly urges her readers to adopt an open perspec-

tive vis-à-vis what she says about her people's customs, beliefs and practices. For example, about her mother and her style of rearing children she addresses the reader directly, saying:

> Reader! Please do not get the impression that my mother's behavior was that of a child abuser. No! That was just the way children were trained in her time. She was a great mother and in no way would she have wanted to make me carry a heavy load beyond my ability.[25]

Yet, despite her exposure to Christian teachings she appears oblivious of Biblical teachings that support the submissiveness of women to men, teachings that served white missionaries in doubly colonizing Igbo women. This kind of gaping hole in the story arc is present again and again in *Ọla Comes of Age*, due to the limited and narrow lens of the first-person narrator. Like the eye of the camera, it sees only what is within the range of its focus. For example, it misses the Biblical opinion attributed to Saint Paul on the subject of orderly worship that casts men and women on unequal positions.[26] In a similar language the Gospel according to Saint Peter exhorts women to unconditionally be subordinate to their husbands, so as to assure their salvation, they and their husbands.[27]

Ọla speaks up against infanthood marriage and the child bride phenomena rampant in her time, which continue to be worldwide scourges even at this present time. Parents decide to marry their sons and daughters with no regard whatsoever to their feelings and input in the arranged marriages.[28] From Ọla's experience, it is evident that a child bride's girlhood is aborted early. Her education is also curtailed, minimizing her opportunity and ability to acquire skills that will be useful to her for gainful employment in the future. She might also be prone to domestic violence at the hands of a husband that sees her more as a child than as a wife. Worse still is that the damage could go on for generations, seen that a child bride that has not been able to speak up for herself, may not be in a position to educate her children to be their own advocates in abusive relationships or to pursue their potentials to fruition in a competitive world. Not only is it a gender issue, partly because there is no equity in it and partly because the boy is usually much older than the girl, it is also a health issue, for when the girl falls pregnant she may not be fully developed to carry the pregnancy or safely have her baby. There are reports of cases of Vesicovaginal Fistula (VVF), due to extreme pressure on body tissues at the time of the mother's delivery of the baby. Her ignorance about her body, coupled with fear of the man she calls husband, could lead to frequent pregnancies with concomitant higher risks.

Two recent Nigerian films tackle the issues of early marriage for girls and the damage to individuals coerced into it. The drama film, *Dry* (2014), was directed by Stephanie Okereke Linus who stars as Dr. Zara. She tackles the impasse in the Nigerian senate when members did not have enough votes to remove a Constitutional ambiguous clause that states that "any woman married in Nigeria is of full age." The film protests against the licensing of underage marriage in Nigeria by keeping that clause.[29] There is also *Wives' Strike* (2016), directed by Omoni Oboli that employs satire to protest child marriage in Nigeria. A group of market women 'sit'[30] on their husbands, in order to compel them to support the liberation of a young girl being forced to marry a man against her will.[31] These two films compare with *Child Marriage*,[32] an Indian documentary that also protests early and arranged marriage for girls in infanthood. Together, these three films reinforce Ọla's view that infant and child marriages have adverse health, educational, social, and economic and gender consequences on the victim.

Ọla testifies on Igbo traditional acceptance of children however they come in Igboland. The people say that "*nwa bu nwa*," that a child is a gift from God. You do not really own it, but it is given to you in custody. So, a child is always taken into the fold, however it comes. Ǫla recounts traditional views on the sanctity of life, even in the case of bastard children that are often accepted into the fold. In addition, an abundance of descriptions of the joy and jubilation at the events of birth in the story explain Igbo belief in the objective of marriage as that of bearing children. It is understandable thereafter that Igbo culture is against abortion and divorce both of which practices limit the human ability to spread and multiply. Traditional oral literature–folklore, music, songs and lyrics–teach children, give rewards and criticize bad behavior in adults. The narrative voice states, rather elaborately:

> Each folktale had a moral at the end. For children, the lesson was always about obedience, truth-telling and good deeds. Each story was like a music composition and the lessons embedded in the lyrics were either negative or positive, depending on the circumstances of the composition. Bad behavior was abhorred. If a peer in a group misbehaved, the lyrics were satirical and warned the culprit to desist from his or her bad behavior. It was not uncommon to deploy music and songs to indicate a lack in a person's behavior. There were lampoons for poor personal hygiene, bad cooking, gossiping, and such other negative qualities. Whereas the culprit might not have been named in the songs, yet the body language of the singers made clear the targeted subject of the lampoon. That manner of syndicating was popular in our culture; it taught all concerned to be on their guard or face the music. On one hand, our songs on moonlight nights were news items that conveyed messages to all and sundry. On the other, music and lyrics were also used to reward good deeds, impart good conduct, and encourage good behavior. On the positive side, our song compositions were about rewarding good behavior worthy of emulation or to show appreciation for a job well done. For example, a good son that was good to his parents in old age, cared for them, and sent money for

their upkeep and the sustenance of the extended family was seen as a hero. We sang praises of him. Soon, he became the most talked about model of good behavior that other families in the village wished their own sons would emulate.[33]

On the function of traditional literature, G. A. Heron states in the introduction of Okot p'Bitek's *Song of Lawino and Song of Ocol*[34] that writers and critics have used hyperbole to attack European incursions into the continent during colonialism that they see as a curse and an aberration.[35] That kind of stance, however, is not notable in *Ọla Comes of Age*, for Ọla is full of laudation and glorification of the missionary ladies of the Methodist Church ministry and their work in the schools. They teach and guide youth intellectually and spiritually, she attests, at all levels of their formal education ladder with strict principles, discipline and strong curriculum.[36] Again, a hole in the story arc shows that she does not see slavery before colonialism on African soil as it was known to be. Bekee, a character in the text, is spared the horrific travel across the Atlantic by benevolent white slave masters that saved him from his evil half-brother's machinations. The white men kept him back as a domestic slave, due to his frailty. They later manumitted him and sent him back to his homeland equipped with hand-down clothes and other items that they no longer needed, which they thought he could use. Then, back to his village, he became the talk of town, and his age mates emulated his mannerisms and speech, because they admired his white man's ways.[37] However, the reader cannot tell whether Bekee, this frail, effeminate or feminized child also doubled as a 'wife' for the white masters after dark, given the limitations of the first-person style of narration. We are told that he learned to cook, clean and sew, all domestic occupations usually associated with women and females. That is all the reader is presented and is privileged to know as certainty.

If J. California Cooper's account in her novel, *Family*,[38] on sexual abuse of domestic slaves at the hands of the slave masters in the New World is anything to go by and is transferable to slavery on the African soil, then one can infer that the narrator has not divulged all the truth on this subject matter. Some African writers, however, have reported about the glaring failings of white colonialists that practiced homosexuality on their male African domestic staff at the time, with or without their consent. An example can be found in the Guadeloupian writer Maryse Condé's 1982 premier novel, *Heremakhonon*.[39] Pierre-Giles is a bachelor expatriate in an unnamed African country. He is a homosexual in an impossible love, as he terms it, with a young heterosexual Fula whom he employs and tries to keep prisoner in his house, because the Fula smooches a pretty young girl Mariama, a nanny to some children a distance of three villas up the road, whenever he is out of the clutches of his master. The young Fula in spite of himself and sadly accepts the desires of his master for the reason of unemployment; "Unemployment, Sister, unemployment," he confesses to his interlocutor as a way of explaining his predicament. Then, there is Ernest N. Emenyonu's 2018 short story, "A Rigid Code of Silence," in which the thirteen-year old male narrator suffers sodomy at the hands of a white male Assistant Bishop assigned newly to their village. The Bishop had visited their village and during the welcome reception for him had spotted the naïve, light–skinned youth among the group. The Bishop flips for him and invites him for a sleep-over at the bishopric. The youth, his friends and parents do not have the faintest suspicion of the coming abominable sequel to the narrative of the youth. Everyone thinks he is lucky and on his way to greatness as the ward of the new high-up clergy. Instead, he is raped while at the Bishop's house.[40] Azodo and Eke in their 2007 work, *Gender & Sexuality in African Literature and Film*[41] state: "just because anthropologists and other observers, including literary writers, linguists, sociologists, have never really paid serious attention to homosexuality in Africa does not mean that homosexuality did not and does not exist." They say this in reference to the ground-breaking work, *Boy Wives and Female Husbands: Studies of African Homosexualities*,[42] by Stephen O. Murray and Will Roscoe, who, standing by the authenticity of their research opine that the "Absence of evidence can never be assumed to be evidence of absence."[43]

Ọla reports as well that the village square is a sort of open theatre where entertainment is performed, business transacted, and socialization occurs. Villagers hook up for all kinds of relationships, not the least of which is marriage alliances that begin there or progress. Events are well-orchestrated at the level of village government with families of marriageable girls sending them to the village square to dance and entertain people, knowing fully well that while they are there they could meet their future spouses. To the narrator's bewilderment these marriages between whole families and villages beyond the two people lasted longer than those western-type marriages between couples. Western forms of marriage exclude the extended family and begin with courting, kissing and premarital sex, yet are not spared the scourge of divorce.

With that singular observation the reader is set up to speculate on love relationships and marriage in the future of the Igbo world and other societies on the globe.

Professor Ada Uzoamaka Azodo
Indiana University Northwest
Author: *L'imaginaire dans les romans de Camara Laye*
Editor: *Gender and Sexuality in African Literature and Film*
Editor: *Ọla Comes of Age*

NOTES

1 *Ọla Comes of Age*, 1.

2 *Ọla Comes of Age*, 2.

3 Felicia Ibezim, *The Igbo Women of Nigeria* (Glassboro, NJ: Goldline & Jacobs Publishing, 2013), 28.

4 Ibezim, *The Igbo Women of Nigeria*, 28.

5 Ibezim, *The Igbo Women of Nigeria*, 23.

6 Ibezim, *The Igbo Women of Nigeria*, 29.

7 Citing George Thomas Basden, historian (1921) Felicia Ibezim notes: "A childless marriage brings unhappiness and a sense of insecurity especially to the wife. A childless marriage is the greatest disaster that could befall an Igbo woman." (2013: 29)

8 Ibezim, *The Igbo Women of Nigeria*, 24.

9 Ibezim, *The Igbo Women of Nigeria*, 25.

10 Ibezim, 27.

11 Ibezim, *The Igbo Women of Nigeria*, 20-21.

12 Ibezim, *The Igbo Women of Nigeria*, 21.

13 Felicia Ibezim notes that "the betrothed (engaged) girl usually gives no objection to the marriage arrangement, but occasionally, a girl would refuse to marry a man arranged for her. In such a case, all expenses incurred by her prospective husband's family during the period of engagement would be refunded by the parents of the girl." 2013, 21.

14 Felicia Ibezim, *The Igbo Women of Nigeria* (Glassboro: Goldline & Jacobs Publishing, 2013: p. 21).

15 Felicia Ibezim states: "Unmarried persons of either sex except in special cases such as the ordained catholic priests are objects of ridicule and derision." (*The Igbo Women of Nigeria* (Glassboro: Goldline & Jacobs Publishing, 2013), 21.

16 *Ọla Comes of Age*, 83.

17 To buttress the assertions about Igbo customs, values and mores is, for example, the author references Chinua Achebe, the illustrious author held to be the father of the African novel in English, and his use of a hyperbole in his premier novel that has since become a classic to describe the abundance of food some in-laws served their affine during a New Yam Festival.

18 *Ọla Comes of Age*, 16.

19 Zora Neale Hurston, autobiographer, novelist, folklorist, and anthropologist refuses boldly and poignantly to discuss racism and segregation in America at a time when she could have done so in *Dust Tracks on a Road.* (Published by J. P. Lippincott, 1942).

20 Françoise Lionnet, "Autoethnography: The An-Archie Style of *Dust Tracks on a Road.*" In: William L. Andrews. Ed. *African American Autobiography: A Collection of Critical Essays*, (Englewood, Cliffs, NJ: Prentice Hall, 1993), 113 (pp. 113-137).

26 INTRODUCTION

[21] Michel Beaujour. *Miroirs d'encre* (Paris: Seuil, 1950), p. 348. Cited by Françoise Lionnet in "Autoethnography: The An-Archie Style of *Dust Tracks on a Road.*" In: William L. Andrews. Ed. *African American Autobiography: A Collection of Critical essays*, (Englewood, Cliffs, NJ: Prentice Hall, 1993), 113 (pp. 113-137).

[22] *Ola Comes of Age*, 18.

[23] *Ola Comes of Age*, 101.

[24] Episode 5: Joseph Campbell and the Power of Myth — "Love and the Goddess". June 25, 1988.

Conversation between Moyers and Campbell: Bill Moyers: The right person. How does one choose the right person? /Joseph Campbell: Your heart tells you; it ought to. /Bill Moyers: Your inner being. /Joseph Campbell: That's the mystery. /Bill Moyers: You recognize your other self. /Joseph Campbell: Well, I don't know, but there's a flash that comes and something in you knows that this is the one.

[25] *Ola Comes of Age*, 19.

[26] I Corinthians (American Standard Version, 34-36). "Let the women keep silence in the churches: for it is not permitted unto them to speak; but let them be in subjection, as also saith the law. And if they would learn anything, let them ask their own husbands at home: for it is shameful for a woman to speak in the church. What? Was it from you that the word of God went forth or came it unto you alone?"

[27] 1 Peter 3; 7 (See also Song of Solomon 1:1-3; Ephesians 5:22-33). "In like manner, ye wives, be in subjection to your own husbands; that, even if any obey not the word, they may without the word be gained by the behavior of their wives; beholding your chaste behavior coupled with fear. (Whose) adorning let it not be the outward adorning of braiding the hair, and of wearing jewels of gold, or of putting on apparel; but let it be the hidden man of the heart, in the incorruptible apparel of a meek and quiet spirit, which is in the sight of God of great price. For after this manner aforetime the holy women also, who hoped in God, adorned themselves, being in subjection to their own husbands: as Sarah obeyed Abraham, calling him lord: whose children ye now are, if ye do well, and are not put in fear by any terror."

[28] Felicia Ibezim describes marriage as an indispensable social function for youth and young adults, which should not be delayed much longer after the age of puberty. According to an Igbo proverb, "When a girl passes the age of 'who is your father,' she reaches the age of 'who is your husband.'"

29 https://en.wikipedia.org/wiki/Dry_(film) Accessed 12/10/2021

30 Felicia Ibezim, *The Igbo Women of Nigeria,* "Sitting on a man is therefore the ultimate weapon or sanction used by the Igbo women to enforce their judgments." (Glassboro: Goldline & Jacobs Publishing, 2013), 40.

31 https://en.wikipedia.org/wiki/Wives_on_Strike   Accessed 12/10/2021.

32 https://en.wikipedia.org/wiki/Child_marriage   Accessed 12/10/2021.

33 *Ǫla Comes of Age,* 22.

34 G. A. Heron. "Introduction," in Okot p'Bitek. *Song of Lawino and Song of Ocol.* (African Writers Series, 1984), 15: "One function that traditional songs and stories sometimes fulfil is to enable members of a family or community to step outside the normal restraints which their family rules impose on what they say to one another. In a song, the singer is free to use mockery to criticise the conduct of other members of the community, and especially to deflate the self-important. Such a singer is always likely to overstate his case."

35 A document attributed to Lord Macaulay as "Address to the British Parliament on 2nd February, 1835" states: "I have travelled across the length and breadth of Africa and I have not seen one person who is a beggar, who is a thief. Such wealth I have seen in this country, such high moral values, people of such caliber, that I do not think we would ever conquer this country, unless we break the very backbone of this nation, which is her spiritual and cultural heritage and therefore, I propose that we replace her old and ancient education system, her culture, for if the Africans think that all that is foreign and English is good and greater than their own, they will lose their self-esteem, their native culture and they will become what we want them to be, a truly dominated nation."

36 *Ǫla Comes of Age,* 22.

37 *Ǫla Comes of Age,* 22.

38 J. California Cooper, *Family* (New York, London: Anchors Books, DOUBLE DAY, 1992) is on the ills of slavery in the New World and its devastation and repercussions on the family for generations even on to this day.

39 Maryse Condé. *Heremakhonon* (translated from the French by Richard Philcox). (Boulder, London: Lynne Rienner Publishers, 2000), 103.

40 Ernest N. Emenyonu, "A Rigid Code of Silence." Eds. Tomi Adeaga and Sarah Udoh-Grossfurthner. *Payback and Other Stories: An Anthology of African and African Diaspora Short Stories.* Volume 1. Vienna African Languages and Literatures (VALL) Series, (Zurich: LIT VERLAG GmbH & Co. KG Wien, 2018), 28.

"That night, I went to bed early contented. In the middle of the night I woke up when I felt a hand creep up my thigh and a second person was in bed with me. I was frightened to death when I realized it was the Assistant Bishop. He flashed a pen-torchlight and put his forefinger over his mouth 'commanding' me to be silent in the same manner Maria had signalled me albeit, violently, eight or nine years ago. He put his huge body over me as I lay on my back. I was like one in a trance and recovered consciousness after he shivered and left something slimy on my thigh. He got up, flashed his pen-light, put a sign of the cross on my devastated forefront, and softly said, "God bless you, Foo-Foo," and left the room. In the morning, he was as officious as ever before his domestic staff. I did not leave my bed that morning."

[41] Ada Uzoamaka Azodo and Maureen Ngozi Eke. Eds. *Gender & Sexuality in African Literature and Film*. Trenton, NJ: Africa World Press, 2007. "Introduction: Shifting Meanings, Erotic Choices," 6.

[42] Stephen O. Murray and Will Roscoe, *Boy Wives and Female Husbands: Studies in African Homosexualities*, (New York: SUNY Press, 1998).

[43] Murray and Roscoe, *Boy Wives and Female Husbands*, 261.

The Text of Ọla Comes of Age

Chapter 1

The Village

THE VILLAGE CONSISTED OF RELATIVES by blood living closely together in the same vicinity in compounds in the village. Several compounds made up the composite village. Two moieties of *Umunna* and *Umuada*, respectively male and female relatives in the nuclear and extended families, made up the people of the village. They were of unilineal ancestral descent, for they were descendants of the same oldest male member. They had a kinship system that guided the behavior expected of every kin in that lineal relationship. Marriage was exogamous. It was forbidden to marry or have sexual familiarity or relationship with one another in the village, due to the bond of blood relationship. A kin of the older generation might well have directly and biologically fathered a number of children in the village, but all other males be they brothers and uncles were also described as 'fathers' to the children. The said children included sons, daughters, nephews and nieces, as the case might be.

The same was also true of women. They were all 'mothers' or 'aunties' to all the sons and daughters of the younger generations in the lineage. That is to say that when a woman was not directly a birth mother to a son or daughter in the village, she was also seen as a 'mother' to every other member of the younger generation. The 'fathers', 'mothers', 'uncles' and 'aunts' together cared for and indulged their 'sons' and 'daughters,' who in their turn respected them with deference in a reciprocity. The children learned from their elders from very early age about the kin relationships and the obligations

and benefits that accrued to them, not to mention the imperative of adhering to the set boundaries, rules and guidelines of
the group. *It takes a village to train up a child*, states a well-
known Igbo adage and it applies here. That was their simple
way of existence and survival.

The villagers not only shared a special stream from which
they all drank, given their consanguine relationship, they also
farmed on lands they collectively owned. Farming in a given
farm area one at a time left the other farmlands fallow for a
period of four years. That traditional practice of leaving fields
fallow for a period allowed the land to maintain its natural
productivity by fertilizing itself, rebalancing soil nutrients and
giving forth rich bumper harvest when next it was farmed.
The practice also ensured the safety of the villagers when they
farmed away from their village and protected them from in-
vading neighbors or wild beasts that found a safe haven in the
fields during the fallow period. That was my people's simple
way of existence and survival in the village.

Long ago, before they were born, their ancestors established boundaries lined with hedges to demarcate the farmland of each family compound in a given farm area. The hedges survived years of farming, and if and when they were
tampered with other replacement trees were planted or high
mounds provided to reestablish the broken-down boundaries.
That practice lessened encroachment by greedy farmers that
would take advantage of the poorer ones, by destroying the set
boundaries in order to increase their own farm plots. In some
cases, where stronger and greedy members of a given compound encroached on the land of another compound, elders of
the village answered summons to arbitrate and set the score
right. Farming in the same farm area at any given time not only motivated each farmer to keep up with the farming schedule, the practice also ensured that no lazy farmer left his farm
to be overgrown with weeds. If any lazy farmers lagged behind, criticisms from other farmers forced them to keep up
with the schedule and pace of the majority of the village farm-

ers. Every villager was a farmer and did his best to keep up with others of his kin on the farm. You compared yourself to your neighbors as a benchmark for the level of farm production you wanted to achieve as a successful farmer. *Keeping up with the Joneses* became a watch word. Indeed, farming was their way of life and their means of livelihood and they were proud to be associated with it.

An elder, who was invariably the oldest married man in a given compound, headed each compound in the village. He ruled with love and pride derived from his position as the head of the compound. If the compound got congested, the grown-up sons branched out and established their own compounds. There, they in their turn became heads of their new households. However, the elder, the oldest member of the original compound that might be a father, uncle or grandfather remained the main elder and leader of their extended compounds. He was respected and consulted by the newer and older compounds for advice and guidance as was needed. From a very early age, children in the compound were inducted into the numerous family expectations, which they mastered and practiced. They were adequately acquainted with the web of kin relationships. Any unmarried elder was not accorded much respect and was relegated to a derogatory status.

Nuclear families made up compounds of mostly polygamous families. A nuclear family was a close family in which all the children were from the same mother. An extended family, however, included pockets of nuclear homes belonging to one male member married to several females or at least more than one female. Each close nuclear family sought first its welfare before that of the extended family. Fathers provided their grown-up sons with farmlands. Proportionately, the farmland decreased as the number of kin increased. With each additional son moving out to found his own compound, the farmland became inadequate to feed and support the increasing numbers of the extended family. Hence, sons able to increase the family farmland were highly commended and encouraged to do so, for their achievements added prestige to the family, especially to the name and status of the oldest elder of the extended family. The entire villagers saw their achievements as heroic acts and statuses of symbol that accorded respect and honor to the family. The more farmland a family compound acquired, the more respect it garnered from the society. Therefore, the villagers cherished more the birth of sons than the birth of daughters who, it was believed, would soon marry, move away and benefit their marital families. Given that bride price was high, men who could afford not just one wife, but two, three, four or more wives were highly regarded and respected. Moreover, polygyny was also proof of prestige, prosperity and wealth. Each new wife strove to have as many children as possible, and competed with her co-wives who arrived in the family before her to have more children. Indeed, polygyny in practice did not only change the family status, it diminished its resources as well.

A village increased in size with the establishment of more compounds. As the compounds increased in number, family lands were depleted. That resulted in each family head not having enough land to farm, let alone feed his teeming members. It was then time to seek land outside the family to buy. Buying land from the poor perpetuated their poverty while it enriched the wealthy. Open communication existed more among the relatives of the same bloodline in a kinship relationship than it did between them and members of other village compounds. Movement from one compound to another among consanguine villagers was easy. Every morning, greetings were exchanged across compound walls and emergencies shared and quickly tackled. Invitations were orally extended. Each person was his or her brother's keeper. If there was a conflict among members of the kin family, elders sat down and quickly resolved it before things got out of hand. Children of the compound felt free to go to any kitchen and take embers from hearths to start fire in their own mothers' kitchens. Borrowing from one another was a common practice. Wives, though, avoided being branded habitual borrowers. Every kin compound nurtured good conduct, in order to avoid being looked down upon by other compounds.

The whole village was governed by an appointed head, whose headship was neither politicized nor inherited. It was not an appointment passed down from one generation to another. On the contrary, headship was earned. An elder, who exhibited wisdom and fairness in judgment and demonstrated consistent and impeccable behavior, earned the mantle of leadership of the village. His compound of origin did not matter. What mattered was his character, inside and outside the village. For as long as he lived and maintained the trust of his people, his leadership was accepted by the villagers.

The villagers maintained and adhered to the strict rules of the village government. Since the entire villagers were related by blood, they were forbidden to intermarry or indulge in any form of sexual familiarity with one another. In other words, sexual relationship was tabooed among blood relatives and village boys and girls had a paternal relationship amongst them. Boys sought and promoted the good name of the girls from their village and at all times avoided having shady relationships with them. Outside the village, boys continued to look after the welfare of their 'sisters,' meaning, all the girls from their village, related to them by blood or not. Boys did not participate in domestic chores, such as cooking, cleaning or sweeping. They were forbidden to show their emotions outwardly, for it was believed that boys did not cry. They were reprimanded, if they showed any signs of weakness or cowardice. They were also forbidden to run away from confrontation, especially from their peers. On the contrary, they were expected to fight back. As for the girls, pre-marital sex was abhorred. If they transgressed and were caught, they were punished with stiff fines levied on their parents. Children born out of such sexual encounters were mysteriously handled. At times, the rule was tempered and the bastard child was allowed to live in the compound. If the child's conception was as a result of the mother's relationship with a man outside the village, for example, the child was taken in by the family and allowed to share benefits that accrued to all other children in the compound. The father of the unborn child from another village could be granted consideration, if he paid a bride price, agreed to claim the girl as his wife, and accepted the child as his. The man responsible for her pregnancy had owned up the paternity of the child and did all it took to save her from embarrassment. In such a case, the girl in the family way was deemed to be lucky. If not, she remained a perpetual old maid with no suitors coming forth to seek her hand in marriage. Mothers carried all the blame for their daughters' misconduct. So, mothers endeavored to raise their daughters according to the norms of their culture.

At the village square, preferably in the mornings, all matters affecting the village were addressed and fully discussed. Thereafter, the villagers were free to pursue their daily activities. When village summons occurred in the evenings, such matters tabled for discussion were deemed to be of serious nature. Consequently, only male adults were expected to attend. Special topics of discussion were for adult male folks' ears only. They were not to be divulged to women, who were believed to be flippant and would sooner broadcast the discussion topics to all and sundry. It was also believed that women could not keep secrets. Women have ample opportunities to gossip. They chattered on their way to the stream and to the markets and even while weeding farmlands. Women's gossipy nature often landed some families into problems for which they were fined in the village. Most women, it was believed at the time, could not have resisted the temptation not to divulge secrets about village matters confided to them, matters that included decisions about sanitation, security, land disputes, and levies for the improvement of the village. Other matters dealt with at the village level included setting aside special dates for the major festivities in the village, including the burial of the dead, disciplining of a wayward member and selection of representatives for missions to other villages.

Once every market week of eight days, the women cleaned and swept the entire village community. When necessary, they also weeded the paths to the streams and the farms and disposed of refuse. The male folks had the responsibility of cutting the trees encroaching on the roads that led to the streams and farms, widening the roads, and filling and levelling the road surfaces. The men also improved the steep slopes of the roads that led to the streams for the safety of those who went to the streams to fetch water, by improvising crude wooden banisters. The banisters not only prevented water carriers from losing their balance and breaking their earthenware pots, it also helped them tremendously while they ascended the hill. Once broken, the earthenware pot like *Humpty Dumpty could never be put together again*. Often, to avoid such mishaps, older siblings carried the water pots of the younger siblings over the hill first. Then, they ran down the hill again to fetch their own water pots. It was generally believed that petrified water carriers were more prone to break their pots than the courageous ones. Therefore, every child summoned up courage and pretended that she was not afraid to ascend the steep hill of the stream. The steep hill slope was more difficult to ascend and descend during the rainy season.

Annually the male folks, wielding strong and sharp machetes, cleared the bushes of a given area of farmland to be cultivated. Farmlands left fallow for four years often had bushes that had grown thick and trees that had become too strong to cut. After the men cut the bushes and trees, they allowed the branches and leaves to dry for two or more weeks. That period allowed them time to retrieve sturdy and strong stems that they later used for staking yam tendrils. Then, they burnt the remaining stems they did not need. The women stepped in to clean the farmland, ridding it of unburnt branches that they took home for use as firewood. Once the women were done, the men stepped back in again to make big mounds in which to plant their yams.

The yam mounds were made high and large, for it was believed that the higher and deeper the mounds the greater the yield of yams. A good farmer was measured and judged by the size of his yam mounds. The men expended a lot of energy making the mounds and did the greater part of their work in the morning hours. A given wife, in charge of the husband's feeding at a given time, was appointed to feed all the farmers, too. She brought a nutritious and heavy lunch to the farm to help the men replenish the energy they expended making yam mounds. The quality of the lunch was considerable, since it was customary to hire or trade labor with other relatives. The men preferred to wash down their meals with fresh wine from the raffia palm. The planting season that began in March, when the heat was severe, did not prevent them from keeping to their farming schedule. Planting at the right time, it was strongly believed, made for a bumper harvest. Specific times were allotted for the planting of each crop. First, the men planted yams, the male crops. Then, the women planted vegetables, the female crops, following up with edible vegetables that would be used to augment family feeding during the famine season. Men carried yams straight from the barns to the farms. There in the farm they sliced the yams into planting sizes, picking out and rejecting those that were unfit for planting. Each potent yam seedling must have a spud that would enable it to germinate. Men positioned the yams in the mounds in a way that would facilitate the women's planting of the vegetables after. They stopped after planting all the yams from their barns. On no account were the women allowed to crowd the mounds of yams with vegetables, because yams, the male crops, were priced and preferred over and above all other crops. That was the inter-cropping method of farming in practice at the time.

The villagers tended the farms well, by regularly weeding, mulching and harvesting the vegetables as they matured. The women had the responsibility of weeding the farms and harvesting the vegetables. The men came regularly to the farms to oversee the wellness of their yams and to stake them when they grew lengthy tendrils, in order to prevent them from wandering all over the farms. Yams were ready for harvesting five or six months after they were planted. On any planting day, given that the activities took the whole day long, lunch was served and eaten on the farms. During the months of scarcity, the women nourished their families with their female crops. The staple food at that time was soup made with vegetables from the farms and fufu made from cassava that was planted the previous year. Carbohydrate intake during the farming season, however, was from cassava fufu. Leafy green vegetables, when available, enriched family meals with balanced nutrition. By the same token, carbohydrate intake was reduced, due to the absence of the yams on the menu. Observe that rice, which constitutes in our time the family carbohydrate intake, was too expensive for many a family at that time. Traditionally, only the well-to-do families bought and ate rice. Even then, they could afford it only on Sundays or on market days that fell on Sundays. Families that cooked rice on such market days also entertained their special friends with it.

The New Yam celebration was the festival that went with Harvesttime. The village head summoned a meeting of all compound heads to select an appropriate date for the New Yam Festival. The festivity was to appease Ani, the Goddess of the earth, who enriched the soil, as well as to placate the ancestors that kept the villagers alive during the months of famine. The New Yam Festival was and still is a show of appreciation to Mother Earth and the ancestors, by sacrificing a bloody meal, usually a fowl. Mother Earth and the ancestors drank the blood of the fowl, while the humans ate the meat. Modern Christians have adopted the period as a Thanksgiving celebration in their churches. However, whichever way the activity is viewed, it was a period of high protein intake in the lives of the villagers and a time to entertain their friends from other villages. Growing up at that time, we queried and mocked the human selfish practice of feeding the providers with blood, while the beneficiaries ate the main and desirable parts of the sacrifice.

Wives and mothers of the compounds prepared large quantities of soup for family consumption and for the many friends, in-laws and strays that would come by to visit, invited or not invited, to the New Yam Festival. Later on, in the afternoon, the villagers and the visitors moved to the village square for more drinks and entertainment. The venue was open to all and there were dance displays. Often, at the village square, friendships were started and established as were marriage negotiations and proposals. The day ended with some people getting drunk and others happy that the occasion had come and gone. Going home, some of the friends took away with them gifts of yams from their hosts. The gifts were not mandatory, but were a mark of friendship and goodwill that would continue, as well as a showoff of family wealth. After the New Yam Festival, the men took care of their yams, by stacking them in the barns according to their sizes and weights. In order to avoid contamination, yams deemed unfit to last till the next planting seasons were separated from the healthy ones. Bruised yams were set aside for family consumption. Meanwhile, the women continued to visit the farms, weeding them when necessary and reaping the fruits of their labor.

The village market held once in eight days. Farm products were sold in the market and family needs were bought. People from other villages came to buy and sell in the market. As Christianity gained more ground in the lives of the people, Sundays were not opened for the markets. Nonetheless, some non-Christians, worshippers of Igbo traditional deities, continued the practice of going to the markets on Sundays. In the long run, however, Sunday markets were abandoned altogether. During the weeks that markets fell on Sundays, people visited their friends after Church services instead.

Death was held in awe in my village. There was fear of death in the community, because it was believed that the spirit of the dead continued to have direct contact with the living and dwelt among them. When death occurred in the village, adults sought to prevent harm to the children. They covered the little bodies and faces of the children with chalk to confuse death and make it impossible for it to see them. Sometimes, children from a bereaved family, especially when a very old member died, were whisked away to other compounds until the dead person was buried. People visited the bereaved family, bringing food and staying to help take care of their daily routines. Bereavement was a time of mourning and also a time for friends and sympathizers to help comfort the bereaved. Visits from enemies were also acceptable and taken as an opportunity to mend fences with one another. It was never explained to me why adults were immune to the harm from death from which they sheltered the children. Invariably, the adults knew best how to communicate with the dead and dealt with issues of death in the village.

Indeed, the village was a safe haven. Everyone knew everyone else. The common rules and guidelines that governed their activities cemented the villagers' simple life and existence and helped them hold firmly the bond of kinship that kept them together. Each villager was his or her brother's or sister's keeper. They were ready to stake their lives to protect their village and their fellow villagers.

Chapter 2

The Infant Bride

I WAS AN INFANT BRIDE, bespoken before I was born to my father's best friend's son. I was not born in a hospital, but rather at my maternal house. My mother delivered me outside her house, in a nook in the compound that functioned as the family bathroom. My debut into the world was a joyous event. It was welcomed and celebrated with traditional songs and cheers. The married women in my village, *ndị nwunyedi*, assembled in our compound and expressed their joy with the usual new birth songs and dances, orchestrated with drum beats, rattles and gongs. The child birth music at this occasion was different from other kinds of music for other occasions. New birth dances and music were performed exclusively by the women folk. They exhibited their joy, grace and gratitude to the gods and the ancestors with jubilation for saving the mother from the agony of childbirth. Indeed, their emotions were justifiable, given that many women died at childbirth at that time. The lyrics of the childbirth song spoke of the mother's bravery and courage at labor, her initiation into motherhood, and hope for a bright future for the newborn to grow up and take care of the parents in old age, especially the mother. Every woman in the village came to share in the joy at such an occasion, not always because she was invited. Her absence would have been misconstrued as malice towards the new mother. Motherhood was therefore revered in Igbo culture and was a criterion to hold on firmly and strongly to marriage in the family for a long time.

My parents, especially my mother, had special reasons to be happy about my birth. Even though they had a son, the heir that would uphold the family name in the future, yet they were extra happy because my mother had proven to the entire village that she was not barren. You see, in our child-oriented culture the main reason for marriage was to bear children. Where a first wife was incapable of bearing children, for example, invariably a second wife was brought in to fulfill that obligation. That was the case with my mother. She sought children ardently in her marriage to no avail. Like Hannah in the biblical Old Testament, she became the subject of conversations and endless village dirty gossips.

"With all the money she makes in her trade, yet she cannot bear children," people whispered.

"Do you think that all the love her husband showers on her would prevent him from marrying another wife?" poke nosed others.

"I doubt it. Let's wait and see what her husband does eventually," others retorted.

As the women came to celebrate my debut, they were adequately entertained with food, palm wine, and a special native white powder that they applied all over their faces. They danced till late into the night and had to be reminded to go home and prepare evening meals for their families. They left, unwillingly though, to meet their marital obligations to their families. They cut short their merriment to go home and ensure that the evening meals were prepared and served to members of their families, and to provide the head of the family and the elderly their usual hot baths before bed, hot baths believed to heal their aching joints and bones.

Meanwhile, the childbirth merriment continued the following day and for many more days after I was born. Many people came from other villages to share in the joy of my family. Each visitor that came shook the tiny hands of the new infant. In some cases, they lifted up the infant for an embrace. I have often wondered how the infants managed to survive the ordeal they were put through by these visitors. I imagine that was their way of showing their heart-felt joy. As though embracing the infant was not enough contact, many visitors spoke directly into the face of the newborn to bless it. There was no practice of hygiene. Unwashed hands from the farms, hands from the playgrounds, and even hands of the sickly counted among the many that came to welcome the infant. Some visitors went as far as to kiss the infant directly on the mouth, even exchange saliva from the kiss with the infant! I even noticed that some visitors allowed the infants to suck their dirty fingers. Looking back on those days, I wonder why our people, who then did not customarily kiss their beloved wives and husbands, kissed infants. How infants were able to survive such unhygienic ordeals is beyond imagination. Infant survival in those days defied all present-day medical theories on health and hygiene. I should rather say that the unhygienic practices of the time helped infants acquire strong immunity from the environment. Infants were given their bath three times a day and were rubbed with white chalk to keep them cool and clean. Afternoon bath kept them cool from the harsh heat of the sun, while the white chalk kept their skin soft and cool. Some said the white chalk helped prevent heat rashes, too.

But to return to when I was born: As was customary at the time, a special local female nurse, who claimed to know the anatomy of my genitals, was invited to perform excision on me eight days after my birth. Her sole 'scalpel' was a crude blade fashioned by a local blacksmith. The surgical procedure, a veritable hit-or-miss, was risky and as likely to be successful as not to be. Often, during such operations, the wrong parts of the female genitalia were hacked away. Some unfortunate girls have bled to death after their butchering at the hands of the quack practitioners. Let truth be told, in our culture at the time, it was believed that whosoever did not survive the excision was not meant to live. Consequently, practitioners were never brought to book. There was no such thing as malpractice at the time. The local midwives were limited in their knowledge. They had no remedy for excessive bleeding or knowledge of the function of the female genitalia. It was believed that uncircumcised girls would grow up as sex maniacs, chasing boys for sexual relationship. That belief, of course, was not true, for there were circumcised girls who nonetheless were sexually charged. Thank God, I was one of the fortunate survivors of excision. My mother told me that she treated my wound with palm kernel oil until it was healed. After my excision, I had my ears pierced. Needles for the ear piercing were used as they came, meaning, they were unsterilized. First, the needle was threaded. Second, a mark was made where the piercing should go. Third, the threaded needle was pulled through the pierced ear at the mark, leaving in the thread. Finally, both ends of the thread were knotted, in order to keep the thread in place. Again, palm oil, the panacea for all wounds, was used to treat the scar.

Going by today's standards of hygiene, one could say that all the unhygienic practices of lore did defy modern medical practices and theories. How else does one explain the high rate of infant mortality of the past, if not to attribute it to the crude medical practices of the time? At that time, our people believed strongly that everyone had a *chi*, meaning, his or her personal god or protective angel that determined whether you lived or died. Your *chi* or personal god mattered in your life. However, all personal gods were not equal, for some personal gods were more powerful than other personal gods. People hoped and wished that their personal gods were strong enough to protect them from all manners of peril and danger.

But to return to my betrothal in infancy: My father's best friends from a nearby village were among those that came to visit after I was born. They came partly to rejoice with my parents and partly to claim me as their son's prospective wife, according to an arrangement between their family and ours before I was born. Well, their son was at least old enough to understand his parents' wishes. But, think of poor me! I was a helpless package, with no input in the arrangement. Some money dropped in my drinking cup was all they needed to substantiate their claim on me. By that gesture, they had *put me on a lay-away*. Thenceforth, I was off limits to other suitors that might wish to come forward and ask for my hand in marriage. My parents were overjoyed by this arrangement, for it depicted their family as worthy. They also had hopes of benefits that would accrue to them from the relationship with their in-laws for many years to come. To further cement their claim on me, the in-laws came on every festive occasion in our village bearing many gifts, as well as jars of palm wine they offered to my father for his consumption and to share with his friends. My father bragged to all that cared to listen that his daughter was espoused into a prestigious family. My father's friends held him in high regard and wished his kind of luck would come their way, too. Thus, I grew up believing that I was already married. That was a rightful assumption, for there was no way I could have changed the situation, had I even tried. Yes, indeed, everyone in the village labeled me as married, even while still living in my maternal home. That affiancing denied me my childhood and kept me on a leash. I dare any modern-day psychologist to analyze the practice of infant betrothal and affirm an adequate understanding of its horrendous effects on the victim's character, in this instance, mine. Had psychologists existed at the time and dared to carry out any such studies, they would have met strong opposition in the village. In those days, the villagers would have driven them out of their community.

My so-called husband showered me with gifts, presents which I senselessly accepted and arrogantly showed off and bragged about to my peers. My peers became envious of me and most of them wished they were in my shoes. Their sentiments further flattered my ego. Have I mentioned that the man was old enough to be my father? Yes, he was that much older than I was. That did not matter, for it was believed that the older a man was the better he could take care of his wife.

That man monitored my every move, made decisions about which schools I attended and what clothes I wore. He directed my affairs with a remote control. He always warned my parents whenever he thought fit to do so. I began to resent some of those controls as I grew up. I often asked myself why I was in that predicament, especially when I saw how free my mates were. The answer to my question was redundant, for the faces of my friends jealous of my so-called good luck and wishing they were in my shoes said it all. You're the lucky girl! Their reactions further added to my confusion. At that time in the culture of my people, it was a prestigious act and a reflection on the family status, image, economic and social standing for a young girl to be engaged. Well, for my part, I had mixed feelings about my predicament at the time. My emotions oscillated between confusion and elation and vanity each time he showered presents on me. What else did I know except the reactions of my peers? Some of the presents he sent were not available locally in our village. He was already working and earning a good salary. He wanted his wife-to-be to stand out among her peers. Was that a bad thing? Was it? Nope! Not really. Sometimes, I fantasized about those gifts. I made up speeches in my mind and presented them to my peers and friends. How vain I must have been! In all those seeming confusions, I still felt boxed-in. To begin with, I was often forbidden to participate in some local activities that I could have enjoyed.

"Be careful! Remember, you're different. You're engaged to be married."

I was always to be mindful of what people would say. I was forbidden to take part in some activities in which my age mates were allowed to participate.

"No, no, no! You can't do that! What would people say if it became known you participated in that activity?"

What else did I know as a five-year old? I felt trapped in my so-called marriage and sought ways to liberate my free spirit.

As I have stated earlier, observe that my suitor handled all the decisions about my future. Actually to describe him as a suitor is a misnomer, because he came on strong in my affairs as a longtime husband would. He endorsed the schools I attended. For every occasion I was involved in, he dictated how long I stayed there. It seemed that he had set up little spies to monitor my activities, little listening posts that reported to him on my behavior, even on some things that I hid from my mother. Earlier, before my school years, my aunt had emancipated me from this ordeal, by taking me away from the village to a cosmopolitan city, where I was under her tutelage and positive supervision.

The cosmopolitan city was far from our village and was a whole day's train ride away. I was awed by the sights and dazzled by the many lights in the city, during my train travel to the city to join my aunt and her family. That was the first time in my life I had traveled out of our village. I had no words to adequately describe what I saw. Furthermore, I did not comprehend the fact that there were other ways of lighting the nights than what I was used to in our village. My excitement knew no bounds. Simply put, I was overwhelmed by the hustle and bustle of the big city. In comparison to what I had seen in the past, I noticed that where the village was small the city was humungous; where the village was dark at night, the city streets were well-lit; where the language spoken in the village was comprehensible to me, the language spoken in the city was incomprehensible, and where the village roads were mere paths, the city streets were paved. This comparison could go on and on and on. Simply put, I was awed by the sights and sounds of the city.

I had to adapt very quickly to life in the city with the help of my aunt, who took me as her own child and treated me very kindly. I also had to learn the spoken language of the city, the Pidgin English that was an adaptation of English and a crude mixture of the many indigenous languages of the city. Depending on the ethnic origin of a given speaker of Pidgin

English, his or her intonation, especially the rise and fall of the voice, betrayed the speaker's ethnic origin. Pidgin English was adopted by all the city residents for ease of communication among them. Here is a sample Pidgin English:

ENGLISH	PIDGIN ENGLISH
Where are you going?	*Wi sai you de go?*
What's your name?	*Wetin be your name?*
You are ugly, or bad	*You bi yeye.*
I don't know.	*A no sabi.*
What is your problem?	*Wetin de worry you?*

Pidgin English helped the diverse populations of the city communicate effectively with one another. It also toned down the differences between the various cultural groups, languages and dialects that made up the city. I soon settled down amicably with my aunt, her husband and his second wife. My aunt adopted me as her own child, given that she bore no children of her own. She was able to tell off the man who claimed me from an early age as his wife. I have very positive memories of those past years. My being a young child in that new family went with the obligation to do most of the family chores. The adage, *spare the rod and spoil the child* was in force and was practiced. The child did all the menial jobs in the home, ran all the errands, and did the general cleaning of the house. The problem I had was that being a rural village girl with no prior exposure to city life I had to learn everything in a hurry or face the tail end of the rod. The experience was like learning to speak and comprehend French from a manual. Reader! That was just how things were in those days. So, please do not misinterpret my narrative. I had the responsibility to wake up early in the morning and start a fire for cooking the family breakfast. I extremely dreaded this particular chore, especially in the rainy season, when the wet firewood went away to Neverland to visit its aunt, as my people would say. The firewood would refuse to ignite and burned with difficulty when it managed to do so. Whenever possible, I collected embers from neighbors' fires and blew my fire until the firewood ignited. The neighbors all believed that I was an obedient child, not a troublemaker in the yard, and so never refused me the favor of taking fire from their kitchen.

The housing arrangement in the city differed from the housing arrangement in village compounds. Most families in the city, including the one I lived in, could only afford one or two rooms of the landlord's house. The floor plan of most city houses was the same. A long corridor separated rooms on one side from rooms on the other side, and separated tenants living on one side of the corridor from tenants living on the opposite side. This type of rooming-house was popularly known as *Face-me-I-Face-you*, because the corridors were meeting grounds for the tenants that must use it to either enter or exit their rooms. Cross ventilation was never considered in the floor plan. Windows were very small, ineffective and located only on one side of the rooms. The windows were often closed, due to the menace from the mosquitoes. The doors and windows were often closed, because tenants protected their privacy and did not want other tenants to spy on them or see how they arranged their rooms. Nonetheless, most room arrangements inside were the same. A long curtain that functioned as a room divider and screen cordoned off a mini master bedroom for the husband and wife, leaving the other part for use as a sitting room, storage and children's bedroom. At night, children slept on mats on the floor.

My morning duties included boiling water for bath for all members of the family, and for their tea, if they chose. After I put the water on the fire to boil, I quickly swept our assigned portion of the yard, and collected and disposed of the garbage. Then, I awaited instructions from my aunt on what to serve for breakfast. Each morning after I had done the household chores, my aunt who traded in the city market sent me to carry her wares to the market, set them up for the day's sales, and run back to the house to get ready for school. After school, I ensured that all the ingredients for the evening meal preparation were processed. I shelled, peeled and pounded all that was needed to facilitate the preparation of the meal.

I was very happy living in the city away from our village, because my aunt showered me with every good thing a child of my age needed. I was registered in a good school affiliated with the Methodist Church, the Christian denomination to which we adhered. My aunt bought me many new clothes, such that I always dressed like a princess. I had many clothes for different occasions, unlike when I lived in the village where parents struggled to buy new clothes for children and could do so only at Christmas. Expert seamstresses made my clothes in the city and they fitted me very well. My aunt always wore an infectious smile that made me always appreciative of her love for me and of my transformation in the city.

Although I was very happy, I ran away from our house one day that I felt I could not have my way. The problem was that I wanted to take along my aunt's wares on my way to school for delivery at the market, rather than return home after the delivery of the wares to get ready to go to school. I wanted to avoid making the trip twice when I could merge both into one, sort of *kill two birds with one stone*. In my humble way of thinking, I felt it was a waste of my time and effort to do otherwise, since the market was on my way to school. To take the wares first to the market, return to the house, and then go to school, as my aunt insisted, seemed to me to be a waste of my time and effort. I refused to obey her, ran away and hid myself at the railway station. My intention was to catch the first train I could get and head back to my parents in the village. My aunt and family searched for me in all places they thought I could have been hiding. Alas! Hunger drove me out of my hiding place. A railway worker took a quick look at me and could decipher that something was amiss. He nabbed me. Although my aunt was relieved that I had been found, yet she reprimanded me and reported me to our school headmaster, who could not believe that I could act in such a manner. He gave me the dreaded six strokes of his cane and made me promise never again to repeat such misbehavior. The most humiliating part of my punishment was the shame of being stood in front of the whole class. My classmates were told of my transgression and I was described as a disobedient child. I was utterly ashamed and my self-esteem dropped to rock bottom. For days after, I could not take the ridicule of my classmates. The incident taught me an unforgettable lesson in my young life; never disobey your guardian. Looking back now to what I did, I still feel that my decision to make one trip rather than two trips was the wiser one.

During the long holidays, my aunt took me back to the village, where once again I was viewed as a special girl and a visitor from the city. My siblings did not even know how to interact with me anymore, due to the changes they had observed about me. For one thing, my mode of dressing had changed. I was always neatly dressed, while most of my siblings still ran around naked. For another thing, my manners had also changed. Above all, I spoke to them in Pidgin English, which they could not understand. All ideas about my betrothal faded from my memory. My mother was very proud of me. She had noticed the way I carried myself. She took note of my aunt's good report about me. My aunt had me educated and she raised me well. She praised me when I was a good girl and behaved well and reprimanded me when I was a bad girl and misbehaved. My ego soared high again. My peers marveled at my luck, my well-tailored dresses, my language expression in English, and my general comportment. I became aware of their views about me, when I noticed their reactions towards me. My siblings, in particular, were so affected by the changes they observed about me that they often suggested that I returned to my 'mother,' meaning, my aunt. They no longer saw me as their sister, but rather as the 'daughter' of our aunt. I often wondered about how I got so lucky. Ignorantly, I took things for granted, not knowing that *no condition is permanent* and that my lot could change any moment. But, change it did after three years of my residence in the city.

Abruptly, the good years in the city came to an end. My aunt's husband was running away from the law for a crime he reportedly committed. He fled the city. I did not quite understand the nature of his offence, but we quickly had to leave the city as well. Thenceforth, my life took a roundabout turn for the worse. My aunt and her husband fled from the East to obscure vicinity in the North, where they felt the law would have difficulty to catch up with them. What a sad event in my young life! It made things so difficult for my family and me. The way I saw it, it was the end of the happy days of my life. My mother was sad that she would not be able to see her sister anymore. My father felt that he had lost a caring sister-in-law. I returned to my village, while my aunt and her family relocated. My parents registered me for school in the one and only elementary school in our village. Unfortunately, once again I was in the eagle eyes of the *bird of prey*, my suitor. Once again he claimed full responsibility for my life. There, back again, the raptor dominated my life and oppressed my little person.

My good educational background in the city stood me at an advantage during my elementary school years in the village. I was fluent in Pidgin English, as well as in the King's English. I excelled in all the subjects taught in the curriculum. I was always the teachers' pet, because they admired the rate and speed at which I learned. Although they felt I was brilliant by all standards, I make haste to acknowledge that my brilliance could wholly be attributed to my exposure in the city. That city environment was more conducive to learning than was the village. In the village school, I was small compared to my classmates some of whom were seven or eight years older than I was. Some of my teachers appointed me prefect over my classmates and made me bring canes to class to whip them when they could not learn. I enjoyed being a prefect. Nonetheless, I paid heavily for it after school, for those I punished blamed me for their punishment and planned revenge against me. I could not fight them back, because they were older and stronger than I was. They were also mean and vengeful and sought ways and means to make me pay back for the shame, humiliation and ridicule they felt every time I whipped them. Since I had not been exposed to physical fights, I was no match for the kind of village fights they wedged. The only fights I knew about were verbal fights, fights that were more of exercise of wits. In the village, physical strength counted more than brain power. To prevent the bullying and antagonism, the reprisals from my peers, I always waited for my older brother to take me back home after school. In his presence, no one dared to touch me, for they dreaded his anger and arm strength. Thus, the year ended with no serious harm to my person.

When another school year came round, I was enrolled in another school, partly because our church school did not have classes for all students enrolled in the school and partly because it was lacking in higher-level classes. The new school was five miles away from the village and there was no other means of transportation than your two feet. Every morning, come rain, sunshine or heat, I had to walk five miles through dense bush paths and streams to the school. Fortunately, three older pupils trekked the long distance with me each school day. My parents left me in their care and they looked after me well. In the rainy season, when the rains were heavy, we improvised umbrellas with broad plantain or cocoyam leaves. Quite often, we were soaked to the skin before we got to the school. Where the streams were deep, we waded through them or walked across them on logs improvised as bridges. On two occasions, I missed my footing and could have drowned--given that I could not swim--but for the timely intervention of one of the older pupils that rescued me. Though drenched, I continued shivering all the way to school, allowing my body heat to dry my clothes. Those were the days when going to school demanded a lot from the students; they accepted their learning as their responsibility. I enjoyed those

years. Though I was small, those years and experiences tough-
ened me.

The educational school system had morning and afternoon
sessions. During recess, meaning, the break between the morning and afternoon sessions, we ate the food we brought with
us from our homes. When we did not bring food from home,
we bought from the nearby markets. On school days, we woke
up at cock's crow, which was our wake-up call. In the village,
the rooster crowed at different times of the night. The first
cock's crow was difficult to hear, for the villagers were usually
fast asleep at that time of the night. Besides, it was believed
that it was an omen, usually a bad one, to hear it. For my part,
and this is without any scientific evidence to support my belief, I interpreted the crude village theory about the cock's first
crow to be an alarm mistakenly triggered by either a disturb-
ance or a light seen and interpreted by the rooster as dawn.
The second crowing of the cock was at about five o'clock in the
morning and it woke up most of the villagers. Those that had
errands to run took advantage of the time it afforded them to
do so, before pursuing their other daily activities. Let truth be
told, the villagers had a habit of *early to bed and early to rise.*
They really had no other choice, for there was no electricity in
the village and night entertainment was only for children that
played their games by the moonlight. Therefore, the crowing
of the cock was a natural alarm clock that woke the villagers
from their slumber, so that they had ample time for their
morning chores. It worked for them, for they were fully re-
freshed after their night's slumber.

On school days, we woke up at the second crowing of the
cock and prepared our lunch for the day. It was difficult to
start a fire to accomplish this task and I often smelled of smoke
trying to perform this chore. I later became adept at starting
fires, after having learned to do it during my sojourn in the city
at my aunt's house. On some lucky days, my mother gave me
money to buy my lunch from the nearby markets. When I say
money, I am not talking about coins and currency, but rather

cowries that were the means of monetary exchange in those days. Twelve bundles of six-cowrie packs--a total of seventy-two cowries--tied together with a thread passed through a hole in the middle of the cowrie pieces made up a penny.

Sometimes, we robbed idols of cowries to pay for our food, cowries that worshippers deposited as sacrifice to the spirits. After the theft, we pleaded with the idols for forgiveness and to spare our lives. We felt that being school children and being hungry were enough reasons to be forgiven and our lives spared.

"Idols please don't kill us, for we are mere hungry school children."

Our pleas for forgiveness exposed the shallowness of our Christian faith and belief, not to mention our marked fear of the idols. We often waited whole eight days, a full market week, to see whether the idols would kill us or not. Invariably, they did not. So, we robbed more idols and repeated the same plea again and again. A more daring pupil among us once took a live chicken sacrificed to the idols. We held our breath for eight long days as we waited for him to die. He laughed at us, saying that we were afraid of idols that could not talk or do us any harm. He lived. We were emboldened and took more things from the idols.

At the end of the school year, my father had me trans-ferred to yet another school, which was about three miles away and nearer to our village. We were all happy about this arrangement. I had to adjust once again to attending school at this new location. I was lucky that my father's cousin was married in that school village. Consequently, I stayed at her house during recess after the morning session and had my meals there. Once again, I was fortunate to have teachers that liked me, partly because I was the top of my class during tests and partly because my dad was well-known in the village. As small as I was, teachers delegated to me the duty of taking care of the class in their absence. While some of the students in the class were supportive of me in that assignment, others were not. Envious and vindictive, they took out their bad feelings on me after school hours. I spent two years in that school.

At the end of the two-year period, my father with the agreement of my would-be-husband decided that I sat an entrance examination into a Methodist Girls' boarding school located in another town, which was run by lady missionaries from England. To get there, one had to go by train, motor car or bicycle. The school curriculum was strong. It taught school subjects, as well as strict discipline that all students observed. The lady missionaries taught us lessons in Christianity, etiquette, discipline and lady-like manners that good Christian girls should adopt. In a given term, the school allowed only one family visiting day. My parents could not visit me during the visiting days, partly because the distance was too far for them to trek, partly because the train fare was beyond their means, and partly because they did not have a place in the village to spend the night.

The school Principal read all the girls' mails before handing them over to us. The school forbade questionable mails. The Principal called the recipients of such mails into her office and reprimanded them. Sometimes, she even co-opted parents' help in disciplining their wards. I once received a love letter from a boy I had met during one of our school vacations. The Principal quickly summoned me into her office and for one hour interrogated me about the boy about whom I knew nothing. I was not only punished at school, I was also reported to my parents. When I went back home, my parents gave me the lengths of their tongues. Every student was expected to abide by the rules and regulations of the school or be kicked out of the school. Any rusticated girl carried a stigma. The Methodist Church that owned the school sanctioned all the guidelines of the school and upheld all decisions of the school authorities. The Methodist Church established boys' and girls' schools in many towns and villages in which it had foothold. The majority of students that passed through those institutions grew up to achieve higher educational qualifications and became good leaders in the country. They held good positions in their jobs and exhibited good leadership in all their undertakings.

At this time of my childhood, the man billed to eventually marry me lived in the capital city of our country. He was getting a special training there that would advance him in his career. He could not see me as often as he would have liked, for that would have entailed two days of train travel to our school, where he would be allowed only a few minutes to see me. He did write quite often, though. Quite often, I wished he did not write, for I did not know what to say to him in reply. My responses to his letters were always the same, starting with "Dear Sir" and ending with "Yours Sincerely." He reprimanded me often about the letters I wrote to him, and suggested that I began with "Darling Sweetheart," and so on and so forth, endearing words that I did not quite understand. How could I write such endearing words to someone that was old enough to be my father, a man that was always far away from me? Quite often, I even forgot what he looked like. There was always, into the bargain, this gnawing fear I had of him. The wide age gap between us and the respect we were taught to have for our elders forbade me to see him as an equal. These issues froze any attempt on my part to relate to him as an equal. In order not to annoy him, I did my best to respond to his letters, always saying the same things. My Principal saw no harm in this type of communication, because many girls in the school had fiancés that sponsored their education at that time. However, I did not quite know what the man expected from me. I did feel safe, though, because the principal did not intrude in the plan.

Chapter 3

The Cutting of Apron Strings

AFTER HIS TRAINING FOR PROMOTION and advancement in his career, my future husband was posted to another country that shared borders with our country. I was in elementary six at the time and very naïve about all matters concerning marriage. I was so naïve and innocent that during the holidays I stripped naked as did all the girls of my age and joined in their dances and plays. I had not reached the age of puberty. Besides, girls our age were not required to cover up with clothes. That would explain the progression of the next turnout of events after my future husband's posting to his new station.

As soon as he settled down there, he wrote me a letter demanding that I join him as his live-in wife. I was frightened and shocked. I, a young girl, whose life was just beginning to evolve! My salvation from the ordeal was the fact that the Principal, who always first read all the girls' letters, read that letter from my would-be husband and it did not settle well with her. She did not like its tone at all after she read it. She sent for me and for good twenty minutes reprimanded me, as if I had disobeyed a school rule.

"Look at you," she began. "How old are you? Why would you be thinking of marriage at this early stage of your life? What have we been teaching you in this school? You are endowed with intelligence, but you have chosen to get into marriage and have children that you are not mature to bear and raise."

I just stood there in her office, while tears of agony rolled down my cheeks. Observe that at that point in time I had not even read the letter and so did not understand why the Principal was harsh on me. She looked at me and saw the tears rolling down my cheeks. Then, she flung the letter at me with a command to explain to her the meaning of all of that. I looked at her as I picked up the letter and perceived a mixture of pity and disappointment written all over her face. It was then that the fear that gripped me lessened, for it donned on me that her anger was out of concern for my best interest in the future. Then, I related to her the whole story of my involvement with the suitor and the part he had played thus far in my life. Then, she said to me:

"Ọla, after all the training you have received in this school, you should know what to do with your young life. You are too young yet to get married. You are a mere child yourself. Married and living with him at his station, you will be far away from all the people you have known throughout your entire life."

That was it. She dismissed me. I quietly left her office. I ran straight down to my dormitory. I wrote a quick, one-page, precise, and to-the-point reply to the letter that caused me so much anguish.

Dear Sir,
I thought you said I would go to a secondary school after I finished here.
Please, I want to go to secondary school next year.
Thank you, Sir.
Ọla

He neither acknowledged receipt of my letter nor did he give a reply to it. On the contrary, he wrote my parents, rebuking and blaming them for encouraging me to write him such an insulting letter. Observe that I did not consult my parents before responding to his letter. Then, he took a drastic step that freed me from what would have been an abusive marriage and a wasted life. He asked his parents to find him another wife, as a matter of urgency, immediately. At the time, any girl would rush for an opportunity to be married to him, being that he had higher education and was highly respected for his qualifications. His parents did not take long to find a wife and ship off to him. My parents, for their part, blamed me for writing him without consulting them. As for me, I heaved a sigh of relief. It was good riddance, as far as I was concerned. But I hid my emotions from my parents. My school principal, who had read my reply to the man's letter, also waited for his reaction. Well, we waited in vain, for his reply never came. When I finally told my school principal about the man's reactions to my letter, she embraced me several times repeating that I had been saved for a brighter future. Later, she helped me gain admission into a teacher-training college jointly owned by the Methodist, Presbyterian and Anglican Church missions. In that boarding teacher-training college, I trained to be a certified school teacher. I also was exposed to the principles and methods of teaching and learning. Tuition for my training was free. My parents were glad, because at the time they had many other children to care for and could not have afforded any extra expenses on my account.

After my training and certification as a teacher, I could earn a salary considered good for the time. With my salary I could help with the training of my younger siblings. My father was very proud of me, for I added to their prestige in the village. With my higher education, good salary and my family's good image, I became one of the most courted young girls in my time. As a first girl to successfully pursue modern education in the village, I motivated some parents to change their belief that training a girl was a waste of family resources. Indeed, I became a hot cake for marriage. Many educated men sought my hand in marriage, what with my education, good salary and good family image. The best part was that this time around I had a say about my life. This time around, I knew what I wanted in a marriage and my life. My mother constantly reminded me, though, as was customary, to hide my true feelings in all matters related to marriage. Consequently, I was coy in her presence and tailored my behavior to the expectations of my family and our village. I knew I would be an asset, not a liability, to any man that married me. Deep down inside me, I knew what I wanted to do with my life. The books I read were feeding me with knowledge and were having a huge impact on me. Besides, some strange feelings that I could neither quite explain nor control were surging in me....

Later, we heard that my childhood suitor was not happy with the wife his parents hurriedly shipped to him. He was insatiable and with an ego nourished by his upper-class status became polygynous. Yes, he married two other wives and left the first wife in the village to rot. I have often wondered what would have been my fate had I not gone through the school I attended, not had the principal and the missionaries that instructed me, and not mustered the courage to write him the letter I did!

Later on, when I was about thirteen to fourteen years old, another suitor approached me for marriage. As soon as the news broke, my first suitor sent word to my parents and demanded reimbursement for all the expenses he incurred on my behalf. And he wanted the repayment done with dispatch. A date was set to deliberate on the matter. Present with him at that meeting were his parents and some selected elders from his village. Present at the meeting from my own side were my parents, some selected elders and a middleman from my village. All at the meeting were people versed in the settlement of such conflicts, those capable of viewing the matter objectively, it was believed.

What no one knew was that from day one my ex-suitor kept a log of all the expenses he had made on me. He had detailed and vivid descriptions of what day of the week it was, the exact date, who and who were there, what were there, and how things happened on that day. Even the sounds of the fortuitous cat that meowed and the goat that bleated found themselves in the copious notes he set down as credible witnesses of his kindness and generosity towards me and my family. His records of proofs were such that there was no room for denial of his claims. That is not to say that had I remembered his claims I would have contested any of them. The truth of the matter was that I was too little to remember some of the expenses he claimed to have made on me. In such cases, he jogged my parents' memories to make them recall them. Here are some examples:

1. "One day, on my way to the market, I came into their compound and found her and her siblings sick with measles. I continued on to the market, where I bought a bottle of lotion or some kind of medication and instructed her mother on how to use it. Cost of the lotion (in cowries)."

2. "One Christmas day, I bought fabrics for her dresses and a box of chocolate for her. She told me she did not like chocolate. I asked her to give it to her friends. How could she claim to have forgotten such an occurrence?"

3. "Once, I was traveling to the village by train from my place of work. Their principal allowed her to meet me at the railway station, which she did, of course. There, I gave her some provisions and the left-over food in my food flask. Total cost (in cowries). She was very excited about her provisions and she took them back to the dormitory to share with her friends. How could she possibly have forgotten that day?"

There were many things on his list and in each case I was asked to verify the expense. I admitted those that were made to me directly, I mean those that I remembered. When all were totaled, my poor parents could not believe their ears and the heavy amount involved. They were shocked. All other people present at the meeting were also shocked and looked on in utter disbelief. Some of them told my parents that they should count themselves lucky to be rid of the grip of such an in-law.

The customary practice was that my parents would be obligated to pay back all the expenses, after they had been objectively considered by all present. My father's fear and concern was how to afford the astronomical back payment for all the expenses accumulated over eleven years of my young life. All invited were asked to look into the matter. Those that had vested interest in the matter were asked to leave the room, so that the arbitrators could deliberate. The arbitrators took two hours to deliberate and when they came back into the meeting place all eyes were on them. My parents prayed for a miracle to save them from the ordeal. Like a jury in a court case, the arbitrators chose a spokesperson that would be diplomatic. His role was more like that of an attorney giving his closing remarks, except that he would not be paid for his legal briefs.

By way of introduction, the spokesperson first gave a parable of two dogs playing together and taking turns to fall down for each other. Then, after the preamble, he returned to the case at hand, adding that in like manner as the dogs the relationship of in-laws was meant to be a friendly one between two families ready to fall for each other. Then he continued:

> The in-law relationship in this case started with friendships that were sustained with visits exchanged between the two families. Where one in-law gave gifts the other reciprocated with entertainment, including food, drinks and various other means to make the in-laws feel welcomed in their home. You made very many visits over the years to see your bride-to-be and on each occasion you were received kindly and were lavishly entertained. Your in-laws did not write down their costs nor did they ask you to pay back their expenses. By jumping into the life of this young girl at her early age, you blocked her chances of having other suitors. Our decisions, therefore, are as follows:
>
> 1. You will not be paid the full total amount of all the expenses you have listed here.

2.   Your in-laws will not make demands for reimbursement from you of their expenses to entertain you.

3.   Your in-laws will refund you only one-third of the cost of all the expenses you have listed here. Remember that the costs you have quoted have not been checked or verified. You are lucky to have dealt with honest people that did not challenge any of your claims."

On hearing the verdict the suitor hit the roof. He cursed everyone, young and old alike. He claimed that everyone--except his people--had been bought over by my father. An elderly man in the group chided him for his rants, accusing him of projecting his thoughts and behavior unto them. A barrage of insults from the opposing sides of the people assembled ensued, so much so that I wanted to disappear into the ground. The middleman sprang into action as his role demanded. He went from one group to the other and tried to quell the commotion. The arbitrators rose in anger and threatened to leave. They could not take the insults anymore. But, they were entreated to calm down, stay and finish their task. They stood by their decision, nonetheless, adding that if my ex-suitor disagreed with it he should find himself other elders to arbitrate his case. His henchmen continued to protest. But, after a while, they consulted with one another and decided to go along with the arbitrators' decision. My would-have-been husband, still going ballistic, left the room while cursing all present. The disappointed party told him that if his behavior was indicative of the quality of his education then they did not want any of it for their offspring. Observe that throughout the whole encounter he did not say a word to me or acknowledge my presence. Throughout his entire life, my would-have-been husband was a controversial person that believed he knew it all, everything. After the arbitrators' verdict he looked for various ways to take revenge on my family, but he failed each time. Little did I know all that time the mess I was in until later in my life! Yes, finally, I was glad to proclaim aloud when I *could see clearly after the rain was gone,* "GOOD RIDDANCE!"

Indeed, my childhood days were memorable, especially after I escaped from the grip of the suitor of my infanthood betrothal. I especially cherished the moonlight nights spent in the village square exchanging folklores and learning dance steps to perform during festivities. The exchange of folklores and the composition of music were part of the games I enjoyed. My people liked to tell stories and sing songs and they respected the art of storytelling, because folklore was a huge part of their night life. Storytellers were in hot demand in the village. Folklores highlighted and explained some events that beat the imagination. They also made life bearable for those that often waited anxiously for rewards for their patience and good deeds. As the people listened to the oral stories they learned them so well that they became experts in retelling their own versions of them to other people. Often, in their desire to surpass their predecessors, they added more details that made their versions of the stories more interesting to their listeners.

Each folktale had a moral at the end. For children, the lesson was always about obedience, truth-telling and good deeds. Each story was like a music composition and the lessons embedded in the lyrics were either negative or positive, depending on the circumstances of the composition. Bad behavior was abhorred. If a peer in a group misbehaved, the lyrics were satirical and warned the culprit to desist from his or her bad behavior. It was not uncommon to deploy music and songs to indicate a lack in a person's behavior. There were lampoons for poor personal hygiene, bad cooking, gossiping, and such other negative qualities. Whereas the culprit might not have been named in the songs, yet the body language of the singers made clear the targeted subject of the lampoon. That manner of syndicating was popular in our culture; it taught all concerned to be on their guard or face the music. On one hand, our songs on moonlight nights were news items that conveyed messages to all and sundry. On the other, music and lyrics were also used to reward good deeds, impart good conduct, and encourage good behavior. On the positive side, our song compositions were about rewarding good behavior worthy of emulation or to show appreciation for a job well done. For example, a good son that was good to his parents in old age, cared for them, and sent money for their upkeep and the sustenance of the extended family was seen as a hero. We sang praises of him. Soon, he became the most talked about model of good behavior that other families in the village wished their own sons would emulate.

In my village, everybody knew everybody else and interacted with one another almost on a regular basis. Villagers crossed one another in the mornings, afternoons and evenings on the way to the streams and farms or to fetch firewood from the bushes. The villagers even ran into one another regularly in the morning on their way to public latrines, in the church and at the village square. Each place and everywhere they met conversations invariably ensued. The younger person would greet the older person with respect, along with inquiries after the health and welfare of other family members. The villagers had tremendous intimate relationship with one another. They farmed in the same areas left fallow for years during the farming season. The fallow method of farming gave them needed protection from danger and harm and exposed them to shared-ways of cultivation. It also prevented some greedy ones from encroaching on other peoples' lands.

Families lived in compounds, according to their wealth and size. The size of the compounds reflected the wealth and resources of the compounds. For example, our compound was a big one, because my father had five wives and a teeming number of children born into it. My father lived in his own house apart from his wives. His house was strategically located near the entrance that led into the compound. Each wife got her own separate house after first living with my mother's mother-in-law or, as the case might be, my father's senior wife. My mother being the first wife and the senior wife lived with some of the newer wives after the death of her mother-in-law. All things considered, the arrangement was for a short period of time, not much longer than one year or two years.

That relatively short period of time cohabitation of the new wife with the senior wife was a time of apprenticeship. The new wife was taught by the mentor and she learned wife craft from her as it applied to her marital family. In the curriculum were the mode of dressing of a married woman, preferred foods of the husband, and cooking methods and etiquette of serving foods to older members of the family. It was not uncommon for a given new wife to resent the many expectations and demands of her period of apprenticeship, especially if they differed greatly from what her own mother had taught her. The brilliant new wife might very subtly and alluringly ask our father to allow her to start her own kitchen. No matter how beautiful and desirable the new wife was, though, father always handled the matter in such a way as not to upset the first and senior wife, whose input in the matter was imperative. Depending on the new wife's request to father, her strategy of presenting her case to him, and how mother's input was sought and acquired, the permission requested to start her own kitchen might or might not be granted. In one particular case, mother could not wait to be rid of the newest wife, whom she claimed was disrespectful, lazy and ill-mannered. Mother informed father that his newest bride was ready to be on her own, even though she knew that that was not the case. Of course, when the newest wife did establish her own kitchen--according to our cultural speak--she was a total failure. We refused to visit her or fetch water for her and refrained from eating her cooking. Soon enough, when it was her turn with father and to cook for him, father noticed she was a poor cook. He took out his frustrations on my mother and asked her to find him better food to eat. He blamed mother for the wife's shortcomings, for not having trained her well. Mother did not care a hoot about father's rebuke. Inwardly, she was happy that the insolent and disrespectful wife had been discovered.

She was glad that father had found out himself what a spoiled brat he brought in as a young wife. As for us, we felt she deserved what she got for causing problems for our mother. As our mother's offspring, we naturally sided with her and were in solidarity with her. Truth be told, we often wallowed in sadness at mother's constant humiliation at the hands of the newer wives and our father. However, in another case, in which the new wife related well with mother and us, we were sorry to see her go. We loved her dearly. We got so attached to her and she to us that she requested to stay longer with mother. The good relationship between us was such that when she had her own children we saw them as our mother's children, not merely as half brothers and sisters. We related to them more positively than we did with our other half siblings from our father's other wives.

As the first wife and the senior wife, mother had the biggest of all the wives' houses and her house had the most number of rooms. My two brothers shared a room, where they also slept at night. I shared another room with my two sisters. My sisters and I loved to cuddle on mats laid out on the floor. At night, we slept like puppies and enjoyed the company of one another.

Father's house, strategically located near the main entrance to the compound, enabled him to censor all visitors into the compound. In some cases, he refused them entry into the compound. Father's position in the compound was like that of a shelter for all the occupants of his domain. In my father's compound, there was an open space in the middle, where our family gathered for special activities and chores, and to share pleasantries with one another. The compound was a mini playground for the children and a classroom where the adults taught the younger children the folklores of the village. In addition, this open space was also a forum for the wives to share goods from their common husband, such as yam rations. It was exclusively the responsibility of the children and the younger wives to maintain the open space and keep it clean at all times. Wives of the compound also met there to settle their differences and to start and settle disputes among their children. If the younger wives felt disgruntled with mother, for unfair treatment, they aired their discontents in that open space. Mother listened, explained herself and her decisions or reprimanded them for their slacks. It all depended on the issue on the table. Mother might or might not be able to defend herself always to their satisfaction. In cases when an amicable settlement could not be reached, father was called upon to step into the matter. Often, though, he abstained from obliging the younger wives, no matter how strong their case was. The truth of the matter was that father, like most men, did his best to stay out of wives' affairs.

Men often refrained from dabbling into women's affairs, for their views had a chance to please one of the parties involved in the dispute and displease the other party. Although at the time men claimed they controlled their women, the reality was quite different. Another type of dispute in some family compounds was that of half siblings versus half siblings. Children of the first wife might have a dispute with children of the second wife. The dispute might be of various proportions and might drag their mothers into it, sometimes at the intersections of age, sex and number in a house unit. Siblings often fought one another with verbal insults, physical force and intimidation. Such frequent fracas made habitation in the compound unpleasant and needed father's intervention, especially to stop them from escalating to an uncontrollable degree.

Every year, the village celebrated its harvest yield with festivities. At that time and throughout the year, father doled out yam rations to his wives for the feeding of the family. Yam cultivation was and still is the pride of men. It was customary practice for a man who cultivated many yams to marry many wives to help with the cultivation. For instance, the wives carried the yams from the barns to the farms where they were planted. Then, after the yams were harvested, the wives carried them to the stream for cleaning and washing. Then, from the stream they carried them back to the barns for staking and preservation. The senior wife received the yam allotments for the wives and shared them among them according to each wife's position in the family. The first wife got the lion share, followed by the next wife and on and on in that descending order of seniority. If and when the wives felt that the sharing was not satisfactorily done or other disputes arose that mother could not settle, father was invited to intervene. No matter the nature of the problem, the first wife held an upper hand and was always supported by the larger kindred. They protected one another and in all cases adhered to the customs of the village. The intervention of the kin prevented the kindred from going astray. It was imperative to maintain a good family image in the eyes of the neighboring villages. They did all in their power to avoid aspersions to be cast on the family. For example, such disparagements as these were anathema to the families and the villages:

Do not blame him. That is the way people from his village behave.
What is the name of that man they nabbed? He's from, you know where.
What do you expect from him? It's their trademark.
You know how his parents are. Do not expect much from him.

Villages, therefore, strove to maintain a good image of themselves in their relationships with other communities, because it affected their marriage negotiations, land dispute settlements, and trade transactions. No village wanted to be negatively branded.

Indeed, those were the happy and safe days when I grew up in innocence and naiveté. I was happy. I was well guided. I was free. But, good things do not last forever. *Good things do come to an end.*

ALAS! THE OLD ORDER DID CHANGE AND YIELDED PLACE TO THE NEW!

Chapter 4

The Mother

I REMEMBER MY MOTHER, MY very beautiful, hardworking and resilient mother. She taught me most of all the good qualities I incorporated into my own life. Physically, my mother was fair in complexion. Her skin color was lighter than the morning sunlight. Mother was also fair in dispensation of justice. She was the strongest of all her age mates. In her youthful days, she competed in the village wrestling matches. Wrestling was a measure for determining strength among boys and girls in the community. Wrestling in our culture differed greatly from its Westerns forms, for drum beats accompanied the wrestling matches and guided the movements of the wrestlers in my village. In cheering on a wrestler, bystanders considered his or her stance, moves and footwork. Eventually, it was the wrestler able to throw the opponent down on the ground on his or her back that won the game. So, winning was determined by the ability of the winner to throw the opponent on her or his back flat down on the ground. It was said that my mother outwrestled her age mates and also wrestled and won marches against her opponents of the opposite sex. Her agility and maneuvers in sports earned her a leadership status among her peers, peers who sought her opinions and respected her judgements.

My mother was the first daughter of her mother married into a polygynous family. Being a girl and also the first child, her mother depended a lot on her to run the household. At a very young age, my mother became the babysitter of her younger siblings, carrying the youngest on her back wherever she went. Whenever her mother was away, my mother took over the oversight of the welfare and safety of all her siblings. If she sensed danger or trouble, by altering her tone of voice she alerted her siblings to run home while she tried to take care of the matter. Whenever she was out with her siblings she allowed them to go in front and she brought up the rear with the youngest on her back, in order the better to supervise and protect them. That was the nature of her mother's dependency on her; she freed her mother from the responsibility of child-care and afforded her time to pursue other tasks. Mills and grinders were not available at the time. My mother shortened time for cooking meals for her mother, by manually processing the entire ingredients for meals at the house. That way, her mother had ample time to devote to her husband, her other children and to take necessary rest from her daily activities. Mother claimed that those responsibilities she was given early in life, which by the way were not considered to be child abuse in our culture, helped her greatly to adjust into her own family when she got married and had children of her own. My grandmother, therefore, bequeathed a legacy that I embraced growing up in my maternal home.

My mother had many suitors from the neighboring villages growing up. In our culture, suitors looking for wives to marry did not do so by courting them, for that was forbidden. On the contrary, they looked up girls at village squares during various festivities, at the market squares, or through recommendations of reliable family friends. Although mother's opinion was sought in the long run, initially her parents had the responsibility to sift through the suitors, eliminate some and finally select the one best suited to take care of their daughter. Customarily, a good in-law was the one that would not ignore his in-laws after the marriage transactions were completed. On the contrary, he continued to pay his in-laws regular visits and brought gifts with him. A good in-law gave special gifts to his in-laws, especially to the mother-in-law after his wife gave birth to a child. He invited the mother-in-law after the wife delivered a baby to take care of her daughter for a period of two to three months or until the new mother was fit to resume her daily activities. On special occasions, the good son-in-law sent his father-in-law hot drinks, like gin or whisky, to warm his body and soul, to brag about, and to share with his friends. Although there was no science to this claim, the higher the grade and quality of the liquor given and received, the higher the prestige accorded the father-in-law in the village. Occasionally, a good son-in-law visited the wife's village with her, so that her people could assess her and ensure she was receiving good care. Their assessment was based on the quality of the clothes she wore and how plump she looked.

My mother met my father in their village square during a New Yam Festival, where in company of other girls she danced and entertained the crowd. Whereas my mother was not there to look for a prospective husband—that was forbidden in her time—father was there to hunt for a wife. He was completely enamored of my mother. Her dance moves as she bent her waist and shook it to the rhythm of the dance enchanted him. Father was impressively dressed in his white man's attire. With manners peculiar only to him, he stood out in the crowd that fortuitous day.

Father's wicked and greedy half-brother had sold him into slavery at a very young age. His white master could tell by his frailty and his tender age that he would not survive the ordeal of the perilous journey across the Atlantic to the New World. So, he kept him in his house as a domestic slave. When father's white master left to return to his country, the slave dealer handed him to another white master to continue to serve. In his many years of service to the white men, he learned to cook their food, clean the house, sew, and do other chores that were necessary and expected of him. His last master, a Christian, made it possible for him to return home to his people. He equipped him with lots of clothes and other articles he had discarded, which he thought my father could use. His journey back to the village was not an easy one, for he no longer knew his way home. After many confusing directions and turns he finally made it home, but not as a freed man. On the contrary, he was rather a changed person, an adult and a misfit in the culture he faintly remembered from his childhood. For instance, his mode of dressing had changed. Then, his speech and the way and manner he carried himself had also changed. He communicated with his people mostly in Pidgin English, his medium of communication with his white masters that most of the village people did not understand. His attire and neatness made him a spectacle in the village. People referred to him as *Bekee*, meaning, Whiteman. And they treated him accordingly, as if he was a Whiteman. The story about him, a man enslaved and then freed in his own country, spread into many villages *like a wild fire in the Harmattan*. Men of his age began to emulate his manners and communication in Broken English, which was a mixture of our Igbo native tongue and the English. Many believed he was also loaded with money, given his manner of dressing. And means he had, by the way, for he built the first zinc-roofed house in the village! He took to tailoring, a skill that he learned from his masters. He bought land from villagers willing to sell and established palm tree and orange tree plantations. By the standards of his people, father was a first among progressives. He was ready for marriage and he went beyond his immediate community to look for a bride.

Although beauty was desirable attribute in a marriageable girl, character was highest on the scale of important qualities. There was a common belief that you might be beautiful, but if you lacked good manners your beauty was negated. Stature was also an important attribute for a marriageable girl. Men preferred plump girls, girls with flesh on their bones that they could feel as opposed to bony girls that felt like wood to the touch. Well-developed legs with strong developed calves were also believed to help a woman in labor and child delivery, giving her much needed stamina to pull through the ordeal of childbirth. In our culture, girls were expected to enter into marriage undefiled and mothers saw to it that their daughters maintained their virginity.

Mothers, not fathers, taught their daughters good conduct, through open communication, modeling and storytelling. Mothers filled their appointed roles with an eye partly on the prestige of the family and partly on the prize that would accrue to them after the consummation of their daughters' marriages. Husbands were not only happy to take the virginity of their brides; they attributed their luck to the good choice they made of wife and in-laws. Among other things, parents were held responsible for any misbehavior of their children. However, the mother, not the father, was held responsible if a daughter of the family was defiled before marriage. Most of the blame was put on the mother, who was accused of having neglected her responsibilities. If and when that happened, the village women congregated in their compound and sang sad songs of shame. The one daughter's bad act could adversely affect the chances of other daughters of the family to get married, for they might be rendered unworthy for marriage. The cultural expectations of an ideal wife were in synch with the mores of the people. The choice of a good wife and good in-laws elevated a man's ego and sense of manhood in our culture.

My mother possessed all the attributes of a woman endowed with stamina to bear children. Her looks and beauty also matched the criteria set for marriageable girls at the time. She was neither thin to the bones nor fat. On the contrary, she was pleasantly plump with enough flesh for a man to feel. Her breasts were upright and inviting. At that time that brassieres were not available, the shape of a young girl's breasts was also used to judge and define her character. Two breast shapes were distinguishable: the round calabash shape and the cupped and pointed shape. Whereas it was difficult to judge the morality of a girl with the round calabash type of breast, which did not easily sag, it was easy with the pointed breast type. It was believed that if the girl had been messing around with boys her breasts sagged. In those days, it was easy to view girls' breasts, because they went about naked and only wore beads of different sizes around their waists to cover their Eve's nakedness. The beads were predominantly of red and black colors. The richer the family, the more beads they provided for their growing daughters, especially those ripe for marriage.

Market days structured the people's week days. Two half weeks of four market days each made one full week of eight market days: Afǫ, Nkwǫ, Eke, Orie (one half week); Afǫ, Nkwǫ, Eke, Orie (another one half week). Each village had its own market day, when other villages joined them to buy and sell goods and products. My mother went to market on Nkwǫ days. Father marketed on Afǫr days. Every eight days, people met at the market squares, not only to buy and sell, but also to socialize with people they met there and with whom they struck up acquaintance or friendship. The market was also a place for exchanging information. It was on an Afǫr market day that my father heard about a young girl whose market day was on Nkwǫ days. He tucked away the valuable piece of information and waited patiently for the next Nkwǫ day to visit the market.

At origin, market days were designed and established to help farmers and traders alike in their communal efforts to make some money, as well as buy needed provisions for their families. For my mother, it was also a day that she put away *savings for the rainy day*. On Afǫr days, she joined other dependable and likeminded women to contribute an agreed sum of money into a purse that was ultimately confided to a trustworthy treasurer for deposit into a locally-constructed safe made of wood. The small and wooden safe deposit box had an opening at the center of its top, through which the treasurer dropped individual contributions in coins--not currencies--confided to her. Understandably, the box became too heavy to carry over many market weeks, of course. Nonetheless, the treasurer entrusted with the content of the box kept it safely till the end of the year, at which time each contributor received back the exact amount she had contributed over the months. People were honest in those days, for they feared the wrath of the gods. Mother never saw the four walls of the classroom, yet despite her illiteracy kept an accurate account of all her contributions. Each week, she drew a small line with charcoal on the wall of her room. At the end of the year, she added up the several black lines of charcoal. That was how she was able to tell beforehand the exact amount of her contributions and she expected that much back from the treasurer. Proper accountability was the order of the day and at all times the safe keeper, the treasurer, proved worthy of the trust bestowed on her by her women's group. The end-of-year accounting day called for merriment. Therefore, the women shared food and drinks and enjoyed themselves eating meat and oil-bean salad, and drinking palm wine together. At home, we the children awaited mother's return with anxious expectation, for we knew she would bring back some or most of the treats for our consumption.

Indeed, beyond structuring weekly plans for families, market days also had the special function of helping to structure the environmental sanitation of the villages. A day of the week was invariably set aside for the general cleaning of the entire village. Additionally, market days were used to schedule meetings when offenders were duly punished or reprimanded. Men and women, boys and girls, young and old people, all villagers collaborated filially to ensure the total progress of the community. Once a month, the villagers cleaned roads, pathways and bushes surrounding streams. All villagers that absented from their set duties were fined. Older women, who could no longer physically participate in the clean-up exercises prepared meals for those who could. They ensured there was always enough food for all. Although modernity has changed a lot of the traditional practices in the lives of the village dwellers, yet the practice of environmental sanitation has

endured, seen that the current government of our country en-
forces environmental sanitation once a month.

But to return to when father was on the hunt for a girl to
marry: He visited several markets and did come across a few
girls, some of whom he found attractive. But he bided his time
to make a choice, in order not to make a mistake. He did not
only go to market squares, he also attended festivals, such as
the New Yam Festival. During festivals, villages paraded their
marriageable daughters participating in dances and jubilation.
It was at one such parade that father saw my mother and became interested in her. It was love at first sight. Father fell head
over heels in love with what he saw before him. Instantly, he
showered money on mother while she danced. Today, that's
what our people mean when they talk of 'spraying' money on
someone engaged in some form of performance. Father followed up with necessary questions to get all the information
he needed for his next moves. First, he looked for a middleman that knew the young girl's family well. The middleman
would act as his public relations officer and would arbitrate on
his behalf in all the marriage transactions that would ensue.
Customary practices at the time reigned supreme and were
followed to the last letter. Among a girl's attributes that would
attract a man to her were her beauty, her body enhanced with
uli artistic designs, her dance steps and, above all, her family
background. Mother, it was said, was endowed with all the
above attributes and more. Her mother was an adept in body
designing in indigo. Indigo is the root of a special wild plant.
The dark indigo designs contrasted well with her light skin
color, for mother was fair in complexion. Before you could say
Jack Robinson, mother was betrothed to father.

Mother's subsequent marriage to my father, though rapid,
was very successful. But, that was until the waiting period for
her to fall pregnant became unduly protracted. Everything
possible was done to help her conceive, but all to no avail. At
the onset, father was caring and loving towards her, just as he
had learned to be from his white masters. But, again that was

until father's relatives and friends interfered, asking him how long he planned to wait before having issues. Time became of the essence. His parents panicked and asserted that their interest was not to have a beautiful daughter-in-law, but rather to have grandchildren. For a long time father resisted all their entreaties that assailed him, until some villagers attributed mother's childlessness to a curse. They believed that mother had exchanged her children with her beauty and wealth. What a tragedy! Soon, the rumor turned into a lampoon. Women that were blessed with children flaunted their fortune and those envious of my mother taunted her with moonlight sagas. Mother's reaction to the gossips was swift. She took the matter into her own hands and made a decision to marry a wife for my father. My father, who had waited all this while for a miracle to happen, was instantly agreeable to the proposition. He consented to mother's decision to find him another wife, a fertile wife. Yes, the beautiful and rich woman that was my mother married another wife for my father to give him offspring that would prolong his mortality.

Unfortunately, the new wife failed to become pregnant during her grace period of nine months. As people in our village struggled to understand exactly what was wrong in our family, my mother took in and nine months later bore a male child. My mother's joy knew no bounds. The miracle of her delivery of a baby boy shut everyone up. My parents named their first child and first son, *Onyekwere*, meaning *"Whoever Believed?"* The name was an indirect response to the entire village Thomas Didymus, all the Doubting Thomas, about mother's fertility and my parents' ability to bear children. Then, in quick succession, my mother bore four other children. As it turned out, I was the second child and the first daughter. My parents named me *Comfort*, meaning, *"Exonerated and Comforted by God."* A teacher in our village church had helped them to find that befitting name. Their third child was another boy, whom Mother named *Chukwumaobi*, meaning, *"God Knows the Yearning of My Heart and Soul."* The fourth child, another daughter, was named *Mgbeudo*, meaning, *"Time of Peace."* Their last child, another daughter, was named *Ebere*, meaning, *"God's Mercy."* In her innermost soul, mother truly believed that God showered her with cogent answers to people's doubts and questions about her fertility and ability to bear children, comforted her in her sorrows, knew the innermost yearnings of her soul, gave her much-needed peace of mind, and was merciful to her.

My father, for his part, considered himself to be a lucky man, too. He had more than one wife and was not deprived of sex each time mother was nursing her babies. He married many other wives by himself, besides his second wife that mother married for him. Out of the lot only three remained and are worthy of mention here. First of all, the second wife that mother married for him was not able to bear children for him to the end of her days on earth. But we took her as our second mother, for she cared about our welfare and lived with mother for many years. After many agonizing years of unsuccessfully trying to bear her own children, mother's wife married another wife for father. She was determined to see her own kitchen endure through the children born by her wife. A woman marrying another woman for any number of reasons, becoming a female husband to another woman, was acceptable and condoned in Igbo culture. It could be done with the hope that the in-coming wife would bear children for her husband. In this instance, first my mother married a wife, due to her perceived primary infertility. Then, my mother's wife married her own wife, again due to her perceived infertility and consequent inability to bear children. Mother's wife was lucky in marrying her own wife, for her wife bore many children. Her wishes were fulfilled, but she always considered us to be her children, too.

At one time, two young girls were pawned to my father to become his wives in what we called debt-settlement marriage. Their families needed money to settle some land problems and decided to give them away. Father welcomed the families' gestures, gave them the money they requested from him and the girls became his wives. They lived with us in mother's care. We took care of them as sisters, for they were not very much older that we were. Father was considered to be rich by their standards at the time and so could afford to marry many wives. Moreover, he needed many hands to help him with his agricultural ventures. In another case, a wife had run away from her husband to my father's house. Father simply refunded her dowry to her husband and she became another wife to him. I did not quite understand a lot of those things that happened while I was growing up, but they were customs and mores acceptable to and condoned by my people. Mother did her best to explain them to me. My father's many wives added to his prestige. They were also valuable aid in the farm work. His multiple marriages increased the number of people in our compound and I was happy to belong to such a big family. However, in the Methodist Church to which his family adhered, his polygyny did not earn him a good standing. He was refused the holy sacrament and denied membership into many church groups and activities. Those were major deviations from what he learned from his early acquaintanceship with the white people. Nonetheless, he did not regret most of the denials. He was focused only on the gift of children to him by God, children to whom he would bequeath his legacy.

While father exerted total control over the entire compound and among his many wives, mother as the first wife and the senior wife had the administrative portfolio, meaning, the authority to manage the household and assign duties to each wife without which there would be total chaos in the compound. Mother established a schedule that ensured father did not succumb to the sin of favoritism in choosing which wife he preferred to sleep with him. For the sleeping arrangement, then, mother assigned each wife her turn to sleep with the common husband, my father, who was forbidden to show preference for any wife. Each wife was assigned four market days together to sleep with father. The wife whose turn it was to sleep with father was also responsible for his meals and feeding. It was not uncommon for father to complain to mother about the misgivings of a particular wife. In such a case, mother had a talk with the wife and admonished her. Failure of a wife to comply with the rules and regulations of her calling carried severe penalties. Father could refuse to eat her cooking, sleep with her, and thereby deny her sex for many market days. That denial went along with the attendant missed opportunity to take in and bear a child. No wife wanted such a punishment, for each time a wife slept with her husband it was a wish and a chance to conceive at that opportune time. The women at that time did not have any clear knowledge of a woman's monthly biological regulatory cycle. The very bold wives easily overshadowed the timid ones, completely altering the schedule for sleeping with the common husband. In each case, mother did her best to accord each wife her turn and rights. Mother's leadership duties could be summarized in five main categories:

1. **Feeding and Sleeping Turns**: Feeding and sleeping turns were structured over four market days at a time. Mother assigned who fed and slept with father.

2. **Cleaning**: Mother assigned who swept the compound and cleaned father's house. The wife who slept with father was also responsible for cleaning his house.

3. **Rations**: Mother shared family rations proportionately between the wives. Mother got the lion's share, being the first wife and the senior wife, followed by the next wife and the next and so on down the line in descending order of seniority.

4. **Nursing Mothers**: Mother gave consideration to all who worked in the farms, and exempted from farm duties those mothers nursing infants and caring for all the extended family children left at home.

5. **Conflict Resolution**: Mother worked closely with father when aggrieved wives brought their complaints to

father alleging that mother had treated them unfairly. Father invariably sought input from mother and never took any action without first consulting her, thereby reducing the number of complaints brought to his attention.

As the years went by, however, father preferred the pleasures of his younger wives and that new attitude on his part did not augur well for all concerned. In all cases, however, mother did try her best to intervene successfully. But, when she failed, she sought the mediation of the elders of the extended family compounds. Father continued to accord mother every respect her position as first wife and senior wife deserved, although the affection he had for her seemed to have waned over the years; he had many younger wives to satisfy his sexual needs. Gradually, mother withdrew from sleeping with father, for the competition with the younger wives got uncomfortable. She took comfort in the fact that she had the first five issues of the family, adding that that was enough achievement in her married life. She basked in the sunshine of her life-time achievements, which she saw as vindication from all the dirty gossips about her during the earlier part of her married life.

Certainly, this book is not entirely about my mother. Still, I like to boast about her all the same. Mother markedly impacted my life and had great influence on my self-identity. Although she was not educated in a formal school, yet her acute intelligence earned her several leadership roles in the community. In her golden years, she was highly revered and sought after in matters regarding the governance of the village. No decisions were made without her input and approval, because all agreed she had a reputation for making good and fair judgments. Her reputation was such that even the men and the male folks consulted her, especially in matters that had to do with women and the female folks. Although I have modified my behavior to accommodate the many changes that have taken place in my life, yet I do continue to believe in and abide by the benefits of hard work, a value I learned from my mother.

Chapter 5

The Special Nkwọ Market Day

I STILL REMEMBER VIVIDLY HOW it all began that special Nkwọ market day. It was a typical day. As usual, my mother, the hardworking woman, had outdone herself. She had exceeded the amount of commercial food she prepared for sale in the neighboring village market, a large Nkwọ market that served many villages and communities. She was motivated to work harder than most women of her time, due to the profit she usually made and the appreciation of the customers that purchased her food. She was also always conscious of the fact that she had five children to feed, not to talk of the many other mouths in the compound that she fed daily. On the previous market day, we had barely arrived than news about our arrival spread like wild fire. Our customers came trooping to our stall, bringing their friends along with them. Before long, the entire batch of food we prepared for that day was sold out. Late arrivals registered their disappointment. Some of them refused mother's suggestion to go and buy from other sellers, arguing that none other tasted as delicious as Ugo's food. They alleged that substituting a different product for Ugonma's was like swapping illicit gin for cognac! Mother held a sound reputation as a good cook in the market and the neighboring communities, a reputation validated by proof. *The taste of the pudding is in the eating,* says a Whiteman's adage, and so it was with mother's reputation with regard to her commercial food preparation.

Mother always used only the best quality of ingredients available in the market. Never did she use any ingredient of poor quality for her food preparation. Consequently, her food always tasted homemade. Even the village elders took note of her great culinary talent. It was such that when there was an occasion in the village and food needed to be served she was consulted to lead the group cooking food for the event. Ugo's food was always placed at the high table. Well, we did not eat at tables at the time! Still, that is my way of saying that her food was among the first to be chosen at any given occasion. The fact that her food was always the one selected from the group indicated that her food was preferred. Sometimes, her food was reserved for special visitors to the elders from other villages, who judged our village according to the quality of reception accorded them during their visit. In our culture, people ate with their fingers. How they licked their fingers, coupled with the gusto with which they licked those fingers, said a million things about the good taste of the food.

Nonetheless, I dreaded the jealousy that mother's success as a good cook generated among other dealers in commercial foods in the market. Clearly, they resented her popularity and were envious of her success. They did not like to hear people talk about her great beauty and how tasty her food was. Some of them tried to imitate her recipe and her style of wrapping and cooking her food, but they failed woefully. They were not happy either on the days that mother could not physically be at the market, given that she sent a younger wife of father's and me with her products to sell for her. In short, her absence made no difference to her customers, who first patronized us before they went to other vendors. That aggravated the anger of the envious ones, who could not understand how mother's absence did not have a positive impact on the amount of sales they made in their trade. It was then it dawned on me that on such days that mother was absent from the market some of her customers actually came not only to buy her food but also to see her beautiful face and exchange some pleasantries with her. Some even shared their problems with her and welcomed her suggestions for solutions.

Mother was indeed a beautiful woman. Her charm won her the approval, trust and friendship of many, even among the menfolk that respected her intelligence and judgment. In a culture in which women were regarded as inferior, mother commanded much respect and trust from the male folks. Sometimes, I perceived covetousness in their eyes, a certain yearning in their eyes and a wish to have her as their own wife. No one else might have noticed this, but I was in a privileged position to see, decipher and interpret their longing.

I particularly detested one of those men, because of his constant presence in our market shed. He would tell mother many dirty jokes that made me blush. I make haste to add that to talk about a young girl with black skin blushing was a kind of fallacy. But, that man, he made me blush! He could never keep his hands off mother's face! To add to my confusion, Mother laughed every time he touched her face. She never reprimanded him. This man's behavior and mother's reaction to his advances totally confused me. Mother perceived my resentment of his behavior and took time to explain things to me. The man, Agụ, mother told me, was one of the many suitors that sought her hand in marriage. My grandparents rejected Agụ's proposal to marry their daughter, not because he was not handsome — in fact, he stood out tall and handsome among his equals — but because his parents did not have farmlands enough to sustain their daughter's welfare in marriage. They were not convinced that mother would fare well in a poor family with meagre resources for living. Agụ, though, was not bitter that he was denied mother's hand in marriage. His love and respect for her never faded. He was happy to visit frequently, see her once every market week and crack jokes with her. Mother, for her part, seemed to have a soft spot in her heart for Agụ. She sometimes made food wraps for him the portions of which were larger than what she sold to other customers. She would keep Agụ's portions in a separate compartment of her market food basket. Some days Agụ would reciprocate by dashing me some money, a gesture which I ap-

preciated very much. Mother kept their relationship platonic.
When Agụ seemed troubled, on mother's insistence he would
open up and share his problems very willingly with her. He
would also listen to her suggestions for a solution. Although
Agụ seemed to be her favorite customer, yet there were several
others that also came to her shed just to see her smile and to
converse with her. Some of her customers would say things
like these about her:

> "Ọ bụkwa Agụnwanyị," 'she is a 'Tiger Woman,' a statement
> and a praise name that made allusion to her strength of
> character and her resilience as an individual.
> "She's a woman stronger than a man."

I must confess that growing up I resented much one aspect
of mother's character, namely, her drive, her instinct to always
stay on top in everything she did, to surpass herself and all
others in the game. There was that instinct in her that made
her aim for the top, always. For example, one Nkwọ day, instead of the fifty wraps of food that she usually made for sale
she decided to make fifty more. She literally doubled the
number for a grand total of one hundred wraps! She was very
excited about her decision. But, those of us that were going to
process the food and for whom it meant more work than usual
were not excited, of course.

"We need to make these many," she explained, "because I
do not want to disappoint my customers. Today is a special
Nkwọ market day. The entire village will be celebrating the
New Yam Festival. Many from nearby villages will come not
only to buy and sell but to visit their friends as well."

"But, Mother," I said to her as I tried to put my usual food
basket for the market on my head, "this load is too heavy for
me. I don't think I can make it to the market. My neck will
break."

"No such thing will happen to you, my daughter, while I
am with you," she responded.

"How do you know that, Mother?" I asked.

"Well, I know, because I have distributed the wraps evenly in your food basket. Besides, I have packed them in a longer basket to prevent a concentration of their weight, which normally would have made them heavy," she responded again, following up her attempts to convince me that there was no cause for alarm with promises to buy me goodies at the market.

Reader! Please do not get the impression that my mother's behavior was that of a child abuser. No! That was just the way children were trained in her time. She was a great mother and in no way would she have wanted to make me carry a heavy load beyond my ability.

The trend of our conversation was in line with what we would expect to experience on that special Nkwọ market day. Moreover, she knew that blood sausage was my weakness and she promised to buy me some as a treat for helping her carry her wares to the market and sell her food products. I always looked forward to eating the special blood sausage on every Nkwọ market day. On that special Nkwọ market day, she promised to buy me still a longer portion of cow-blood sausage, because she had calculated well ahead of time that she would make a good profit in her sales of the day.

Cow-blood sausage was prepared with the blood of a butchered cow.

How to Prepare Blood Sausage: a Method
1. Cut the throat of the cow with a knife and catch the blood in a container.
2. Clean the large intestines of the cow in the stream.
3. Season the coagulated blood very well with salt and pepper.
4. Cut the large intestines of the cow according to the length you want them to be.
5. Pour the mixture of seasoned coagulated blood into the large intestines of the cow.

6. Tie the two ends of the intestines to prevent any seepage of the seasoned mixture.
7. Boil the intestines into sausages in a large pot.
8. When fully cooked, remove the pot from the fire
9. Take out the boiled sausages from the pot
10. Eat hot or cold. Voilà! Bon appétit!

Take note that at the time cow-blood sausage was the principal source of affordable protein for many people. However, children, especially young girls, were forbidden to buy it by themselves from the sellers to eat. It was believed that once the habit of eating the sausage was formed, if not curtailed, it might lead to theft. It was believed that if a girl formed the habit of buying the sausage it could lead her to stealing in the future. Moreover, when she got married she might not be able to control her appetite and that could make her mismanage her family's resources. Society frowned upon such a girl, who was seen as spoilt and gluttonous.

"Such behavior may be habit-forming and may lead to stealing, if not curbed," adults often said.

Mother had explained all these to me several times, but I did not believe her, given that a girl could never have enough money to buy herself cow-blood sausage.

"Stay away from the butchers, if you know what is good for you," Mother would often say to me.

Each time we went to the market, mother and I, she bought me long-sized sausages to satisfy my needs and cravings. Today, the special Nkwo day, she promised to buy me even more than she did usually, given that I was willing to carry even a heavier food basket for her to the market. On our way to the market she reverted to her usual practice of praising me, calling me by the praise names and pet names that she exclusively used when she wanted more service from me. For example, she would always call me *Nwannenneya*, meaning, *Mother's (Special) Sister*. She believed I was her reincarnated sister that God gave her to come and help make her married life a success. That special praise name always flattered my ego. Today, hearing it again seemed to lighten my load and I walked in faster steps towards the market.

"Let's move quickly and see what this special market day has in store for us. I must be there to buy fresh vegetables directly from the farmers, not wilted ones from the retailers. Today is going to be good for us. You will see," Mother said.

"Why do you think so, mother? I asked.

"It is because of the New Yam Festival. I hope it does not rain, for rain would spoil all the fun for us and for the many visitors that would come to enjoy the day with their friends."

Details about our special day given and received, mother and I set off to the market a distance of about two miles from home it seemed to me at the time. The sun was just peeking out of the cloudy and overcast skies, ushering in the seven colors of the rainbow. Mother saw this phenomenon, the rainbow, as a good omen from above. She forecasted that it was not going to rain that day, adding that from her limited knowledge of the Bible--which she could not read it, due to her illiteracy--God had directly promised Noah that whenever there was rainbow in the sky it would not rain. I was awed by that revelation and cheered by God's promise of a rainless Nkwo market day, as well as mother's assurance to me that God never broke promises He made. She opined also that the celebrants of the day had consulted a rain doctor that had the ability to stop the rain from falling. I took all her words as the Gospel truth. What did I know at the time?

By the time we got to the market, the market square was unlike any other Nkwo market days. Instead of a few scattered marketers at that time of the morning, the place was teeming with people. They were all already there; tall and short people, rich and poor people, dark-skinned and fair-complexioned people, young and old people, men and women, and owners of the market stalls and visitors to the market. The sun that had then risen to its full splendor added color to the scene. The many colorful types of apparel, typical of African wear, added further to the beauty of the scene. Above all, there was the deafening noise from the marketers shouting at the top of their voices as they greeted friends and made extra effort to be heard. Everybody was shouting in an effort to be heard. The noise was not in the least offensive nor displeasing to all and sundry. It was joyful and happy. Friends were enjoying themselves at that famous Nkwọ market, celebrating another year of being alive and harvesting their crops. Buyers striving to get the best bargain for their money's worth added to the event. Friends got the attention of their friends in the market with laughter, nudging and shouting. The market, along with the boisterous noise, had a rhythm of its own, a rhythm that could be broken only by booing when someone was caught stealing or cheating.

As we approached the market, the noise of that eventful day seemed to lighten my load. I could not contain my joy nor wait to be seated and start selling our prepared food. Soon, we were at the periphery of the market. I was worried that I might trip and spill the contents of my basket. Mother asked me to remain where I was, while she carried her own market basket to the shed. Her intention was to return and fetch me as soon as she had set down her load at the shed. I paid no heed to her instruction. Instead, I followed her closely, stepping into her footsteps till she got to the shed, laid down her load, and asked a friend to watch it while she went back to fetch her daughter. No sooner did she lay down her load than I asked for help to put down my own load, too. She was startled on beholding me. She was going to rebuke me for disobedience, but her demeanor quickly changed into a broad smile, then laughter, followed with praises of me for having turned into a brave daughter.

We had barely finished setting out our food than customers descended on us in droves to buy. First, there were the usual customers, it seemed. Then, more and more buyers came and I feared there was going to be a stampede. As mother was selling the food, I was equally busy taking orders from those that thought the food would run out before it was their turn. As the number of orders continued to grow I was bombarded from all corners, so much so that I lost count of who ordered what. Before long, all the food was gone, sold out. Mother counted her money and secured it firmly in her waist bank. Given that handbags were not fully in vogue at the time, waist banks were the safest means of carrying money in those days. Besides, mother explained to me that money in her waist bank was in her total control and no one dared come near to rob her.

Finally, the hour I had been waiting for arrived, the hour that motivated me to carry a load heavier than usual and walk in mother's footsteps to reach our destination. Mother asked me to stay and watch the shed, while she went to make her purchases. It was a good day, because the afternoon was still very young and mother could still buy directly from the farmers, not retailers that would cheat her. Waiting for mother to come back was nothing, because I knew that when she finally did come back she would fulfill all her promises to me. Thinking of the treat she would bring back for me made my mouth water and the waiting worth the while. I also recalled that she usually took a long time doing her purchases. She did not just pay the asking price for the items she needed, she bargained extensively with the sellers.

Unlike other women that bargained for a short period of time or were intimidated by the sellers, mother took her time to bargain. In some instances, she pretended that she had made her last offer and made believe she was leaving only to make some complimentary remarks about the seller. Before you knew it, she would engage in a friendly conversation with the dealer, to the extent that onlookers thought they were long-time friends. Before long, mother would inquire about her children, her family and all the important people in her village. Then, mother would revert to the dealer's price on the items they had discussed earlier and the last offer she had made on them. Obviously, the ploy was that since the friendly banter between the seller and buyer had gone so far the seller ought to concede to the buyer's offer. Of course, that often happened and mother was always the winner in the end. The banter, the extreme bargaining used to irritate me. It was such that mother sat me down for a lecture on bargaining. She advised me to be careful when I got married that I did not waste money paying for goods at the dealer's price. Mother may not have seen the four walls of any given classroom, nor earned a degree in Psychology or Marketing, yet did she surely know something about dealers' weaknesses. She combined all that knowledge, or should I say all that trickery, with a flash of her winning smiles that none could resist. Mother bargained with charm and smiles and complimentary conversations. Mother's charisma won her friends very easily. Still, that was not all; mother would ask the dealers for more after she had paid for the items she bought. She would demand bonus for her purchases, what we call *jara* in our culture.

Market bonuses or *jara* were extras of a given item on sale doled out freely at the dealer's expense to the customer. Hence, market bonuses meant different things to the buyer and seller. On the one hand, market bonuses to the seller were like advertising incentives and samples of products on sale that he or she passed over to the consumer. The dealer used the incentives and samples to retain customers for the continuity of his trade. Some dealers were cautious in doling out bonuses to customers, lest their profit depreciated gravely. Other dealers gave out fewer incentives to customers, but made up the lacuna with sweet talks and jokes. Still others incapable of the wiles of sweet talks and jokes gave generously, in order to achieve the same goal of customer retention. On the other hand, to the buyer *jara* was an extra gain and a good incentive that could motivate him or her to return to the same dealer another day. A good buyer must master marketing tricks or risk not getting his or her money's worth for goods purchased in the market. Mother knew all the tricks. When others compared what they paid for a product with what she paid for the same product they felt cheated and helpless. Father's other wives dreaded to be asked by mother to buy her things in the market, for they could never do it to her satisfaction.

Mother would bring back to the shed large quantities of unshelled melon seeds that wholeselers sold to her with a standard measuring cup. The melon seeds were used in the preparation of melon cakes, which mother sold in the market. For example, she would ask the dealer to sell to her twelve cups of melon seeds, which at the time was worth a shilling. Then, she followed up each purchase with a demand for her *jara*. If the *jara* she received was not to her satisfaction, she would go ahead and buy another shilling's worth of the item. She followed up each purchase with a demand for *jara*. Each deal was considered to be a new transaction. When it suited her, she bought the entire number of cups of melon seeds she needed for the day in one go, and, if the entire market bonus was to her satisfaction, she would always return to the same dealer the next market day. Although she was known to be friendly in her dealings with people, it was not uncommon for her to feign annoyance, even anger, in order to take a brief retreat from negotiations not proceeding to her liking, hoping that the seller would succumb, meaning, call her back and accept *her* offer. Mother was a very shrewd trader and she managed her resources very well.

But to return to the special Nkwo market day celebrating the New Yam Festival: I was still waiting for mother to return from making various purchases for her trade and bring me back the promised blood sausage. As usual, she was taking her jolly good time bargaining to get the best deal in her purchases. I was getting hungry and restless. But, guess who showed up at the shed? Agụ! Mother's favorite admirer, friend and regular customer! I greeted him well as our regular customer. As usual, he was in a good mood. However, his good mood changed to disappointment on noticing that mother was not in the shed. I was annoyed, but greeted him as graciously as my anger permitted me to do. He beamed in response and bombarded me with questions about mother's whereabouts, questions that showed his concern for her welfare.

"Where is your mother? I hope she is not ill or something."

"No, she is not ill. She has to buy some products and is in the market somewhere in the crowd."

"Good. Where is the food you sell? I hope you reserved some for me."

"I am sorry. The food sold out so fast that we did not have time to reserve some for you. The crowd was impossible to control."

"Oh! No!" he muttered his irritation and dissatisfaction.

"You see, there was a near stampede as soon as we arrived. We just did not have time to save some for you. I am so sorry. People came very early to the market today."

"Never mind, it's alright. I have eaten enough of Ugo's food in the past to last me a life time. There will be another market day. We only wanted to see you and your mother. I don't..."

I did not hear the rest of what he was saying. My attention was drawn to a very handsome young man in his company, who had been standing behind him all the while we were talking. The young man came forward into full view and looked at me and through me with his mouth agape. He did not even attempt to hide his thoughts and feelings. His eyes bored through me and were beginning to make me so uncomfortable that all I could do was blurt out a greeting.

"Good afternoon, sir."

Agụ nudged him to call his attention to my greeting. Then, he became conscious of his manners. But, still he focused his full gaze on my immature face. His eyes seemed to dance as he flashed a smile, which revealed his sensual mouth.

"Good afternoon," he finally said. "What is your name?" he asked me.

I was confused, to say the least. Agụ perceived my confusion and came to my rescue with a brief introduction.

"Amamba, this is Ọla, Ọlaọcha. Her mother and I have remained very good friends in the many years that we have known each other. I have known this child since she was born and it has been my joy to watch her grow into a beautiful girl. She is showing a striking resemblance to her mother. You should see her mother!"

The young man was listening with his eyes, not his ears. And my discomfort was mounting by the minute. I managed to control myself, by looking away from this tantalizing stranger and focusing my eyes on the ground. By the way, the young man's name was Amamba, Ama for short. Agụ saved the day once more, by suggesting that they came back another day.

"Tell your mother that we stopped by. We may come back again another day to see her."

I did not see them again that day or for quite a while after that day. But, I had the feeling that they would return, especially that Ama would come back. After Ama had gone away in the company of Agụ, thoughts of him that I would characterize as 'bad', continued to invade my sensibility. Those thoughts caused me to shiver and tremble, as I became conscious of my emotional vulnerabilities that hitherto were unbeknownst to me. I was still lost in deep thoughts of Ama to the extent that when mother returned and handed me my blood sausage I did not want to eat it immediately. Instead, I told her that I would take it home and share with my siblings. Now, that was something I had never done in the past, namely, hold on to my blood sausage until I got home to share with my siblings. In saying so, I had forgotten temporarily that mother always bought some blood sausages for them too. Mother did not quite understand this new generosity on my part, but took the whole incident on its face value. Finally, after our return home from that special Nkwọ market day, we settled down to our regular daily routines in the family compound, Mother and I.

Being the first daughter of the family, I was raised with strict discipline. I had many responsibilities that I performed on a daily basis. First of all, I had responsibility to fetch most of the water needed for family use. The stream was well over a mile and a half away. Walking in the footsteps of my mother, who was full of strength and ability, I tried to carry bigger pots above and beyond my age. My friends and age mates resented me for forcing them to go beyond their own abilities and limits. We would run all the way to the stream, but were careful to carry our pots of water safely home. The hill up and down the path to the stream was often slippery, especially during the rainy season or when one of us fell down and broke her water pot. Sometimes, my father's newest wife, too young to live by herself yet, went with us to the stream. At other times she did go with us, because she did not have too many chores to do or because the household water was running low and she needed to help with its replenishment. She was different from my mates and me. For one thing, because she was older and married, she was denied some of the privileges we enjoyed. For another thing, at all times she had to prove that she was a good wife. If she took as much time as we did to accomplish a given task, she was reminded that she had come to marry and not to play. She could not refuse any chore assigned to her or she would be called lazy. Sometimes, I felt pity for her and secretly helped her to carry out some of her chores. Mother watched her every move closely like a hawk, because she did not want to incur father's admonitions for neglecting her responsibility of making her a suitable wife for the family. Being the first wife, mother had great power over her. She, on her part, respected mother's authority. Living with mother meant working as hard as she did. Mother always expected hard work also from her own children.

Second of all, as the first daughter of the family, I had a big responsibility to weed mother's portion of the family farmland. My age mates and I traded the weeding of one another's family farms by barter. I had joined a group of my age mates that were strong and could do a good day's job. We took turns weeding one another's family farms and we were fed by the families whose farms we weeded. The group also compared the quantity and taste of the food their different families brought to them in the farm. We competed to see who weeded more mounds of yams at the end of the day. For instance, if Chidi weeded forty mounds in our family farm, I was obligated to reciprocate by weeding the same number of mounds when it was the turn of her family. It seemed easier and safer to weed in groups than as single individuals. It also ensured the safety of everyone involved.

Third of all, as first daughter of the family, I had responsibility to fetch firewood needed for cooking in the family as well. It was one of the many events I was happy to participate in while growing up, because it afforded me the freedom to roam around, make my own decisions and let my free spirit loose. Besides, there were all the wild fruits and berries to pick and feast on in the bushes. I looked forward to the challenge of competing with my age mates, to see who would find and carry more firewood home than the others. When there was no firewood around to gather, I looked for some dried tree branches to bundle up as firewood. I knew very well that girls were forbidden to climb trees, but I did it all the same. Up on the tree, I was happy to see where I cut down the dried branches with a machete or pushed them hard with my foot until they broke and came down. The whole exercise of fetching firewood let my spirit roam free. I felt the joy of conquest and doing what I was forbidden to do. This freedom to roam the wild free was a secret that my age mates and I kept to us. No one told on the other.

I once had a frightening and life-threatening encounter in the bushes while fetching firewood. News of the death of a very rich, influential and powerful man in a nearby village had reached our family. All who heard the news marveled at the great loss, because many believed he was immune to death. I believed at the time that the very wealthy and powerful people could not die. From the way the news was reported, we did not understand the implications of his death. My friends and I were in pursuit of firewood a day after the death of the famous man. As was our habit and practice, we were chatting and laughing along the path to the bushes. It seemed that our luck was shining, for our path was strewn with firewood. No sooner did we finish collecting the batch of firewood on our pathway than other batches ahead invited our attention. We were thrilled about our good fortune. We were carried away with happiness. It never occurred to us that it was unusual to have that many batches of firewood so enticingly displayed at one location. Our thoughts were simply to surprise our mothers with heavy bundles of firewood, more bundles than we had ever brought home after only a short escapade into the bushes. I was always choosy about the kind of firewood I collected, preferring the bigger branches that would make and keep the embers going for a long time. Consequently, I rushed ahead of my party, cutting and piling the best of the lot and leaving the thinner branches for those coming after me. I was so fast in picking and cutting and so involved in what I was doing that I did not realize I had separated from my friends. When I no longer heard their chatter and voices, I stopped and called out to them. Then, I relaxed when I heard a sound nearby. Soon, I realized that I heard the sound only when I moved and that it stopped when I stopped. I became terrified. I called out to my friends again, but got no response from them. My heart skipped a beat. I believed all of that to be a kind of hide and seek game we played on one another. In my fear and confusion, I boldly became talkative.

"You can't scare me. I know you are hiding in the bushes to frighten me. Come on, show yourselves. You know that I always take my pick before you. Come on!"

Then I beheld a total stranger wielding a machete. The shine on the weapon's blade that sunny day resembled the reflection of light on glass. Evidently, the stranger had been stalking me in the bushes. But he stepped on a dead branch and the noise at once gave him away and drew my attention to where he stood. I ran for dear life, running and shouting as I did. I dropped my machete in the process. I ran through the bushes not looking back till I rejoined my friends, who were still collecting firewood. I was panting hard as I briefly told them whom I had seen. We ran as fast as we could, screaming as we ran. We continued to run without stopping till we reached the familiar path of our farm, which was safer than the bushes. We collapsed on the ground, panting heavily. I let out one loud scream as I ran.

"HEAD.... HUNTERS...!"

Then, we saw three adults returning from their farms. I narrated to them what I had seen and the reason we were panting. They confirmed our worst fears that headhunters from the village of the recently deceased rich and famous man in the news were abroad in our village seeking a human head with which to bury him, adding that I surely had run into one of them. They counted us to ensure we were not missing any-one of our group. At that time, it was the practice to bury a wealthy and powerful man with a head severed from a living soul to minister to his needs in the land of the dead. Some women also confirmed sighting headhunters. They reported that the ripe ears of corn in their farms had been severed from their stalks. The assumption was that the headhunters fed themselves on corn while headhunting, but left the corn stalk standing to hide their theft. Our village knew the identity of the headhunters. Invariably, they were either brave men from another village or brave men hired to hunt for heads of the living to bury their great men. They often came when the crops were ripe in the farms. What no one knew was exactly how they fared after the crops had been harvested or how they preserved the body of the dead until a head was secured for its burial.

But to return to our encounter with headhunters: Our vil-lage drum sounded and summoned all adult men to the vil-lage square. The matter for discussion was exclusively for the menfolk, meaning that women were excluded from such a gathering. Women, it was believed, were talkative, and would, in spite of themselves, inadvertently, divulge vital information to outsiders. It was also believed that secrets were better kept, if women knew nothing about them. This belief had adherents from both sides of the aisle. Both sexes saw it as a sacred and protective measure at all times, that is, to keep secrets away from women. According to one story, once upon a time, long ago, another village hunted and took the head of a woman from our village. Our village sent able men to seek revenge, after pleading with the gods and asking the ancestors to intercede on our behalf. Neither women nor children knew about the plot. The village knew that during the New Yam Festival heroes of the revenge team danced in frenzy, brandishing skulls they collected during their retaliation ventures as a way to appease the gods and the ancestors. The heroes were applauded, worshipped and held in awe for their brave exploits. All believed that headhunters would think twice before coming round to our village to hunt. Only the adults, especially the men, could tell which skulls were more recently harvested than the others. Wives, whose husbands were counted among the braves, were proud of them. Young girls from other villages longed to be married to such heroes.

That special night, as the big gong of the village sounded, we suspected that the decisions the men would make at the village square that evening would be about the safety of the community. Our guess was confirmed by the town crier, who went around the entire village informing all and sundry about the decision that the men of the village had taken. He woke up everyone with the sound emanating from his big and hollow gong interspersed with directives as to how to proceed thenceforth:

GOO! GOO! GO! GOGOM!
"A curfew will go into effect this night until further notice."
GOO! GOO! GO! GOGOM!

"Everyone must be in his or her compound as soon as it is dark."

GOO! GOO! GO! GOGOM!

"Early risers, who have special errands to run in the morning, must be accompanied by four other adults before leaving their compounds."

GOO! GOO! GO! GOGOM!

"Female farmers must go in groups, accompanied by male adults appointed by the village head."

GOO! GOO! GO! GOGOM!

"Anyone who goes contrary to these edicts would be heavily fined."

GOO! GOO! GO! GO! GOGOM!

Besides the precautions given, able men were appointed to parade the village every night until the problem was solved. Mother did not break any of the curfew rules. On the contrary, she enforced them and advised other wives to follow suit. She admonished the younger wives, if they stayed outside the compound after dark, adding that it was improper and unladylike to do so. Mother had her way of dealing with such insubordination. Often, she kept knowledge of the offense away from father, knowing fully well that if he got to know about their transgression he would mete out harsher punishment to them than she did for the same offense. Mother also tried to maintain the status quo. Nonetheless, she was also well aware that if she constantly reported to father the misdeeds of the wives, she would erode her authority and effectiveness as manager, as well as damage her relationship with her co-wives.

Chapter 6

The Betrothal

TWO WEEKS AFTER AMAMBA AND I met at the market square my parents received word from his parents that they would like to pay them a visit. My parents consented to their request, for *you do not reject an unspoken request*, according to an old Igbo adage. On the appointed day, the day agreed upon for the visit, Amamba's parents came carrying a jar of palm wine. The jar was larger than what one would consider normal size and acceptable in our culture. Mother cooked enormously, as though she was expecting to entertain a whole village. She always maintained that it was better to have leftovers than have to make embarrassing apologies to your guests at the end, if you ran out of food. There were six people in Amamba's parents' entourage; five men and a woman. The lone woman among them was Amamba's mother. As was customary, she carried the jar of wine, while the men came behind her adorned in their chieftaincy regalia. Agu, Mother's special friend was there as the middleman that would oversee all the matters tabled for discussion that day. Amamba sauntered in immaculately dressed. He looked distinguished. He stood out from all the others, dressed as he was like the white colonialists present in our country at the time. He had the popular Bourdillon-style haircut, which was in vogue among the educated youths at the time. I was convinced that the group was there for a special purpose, seen the essential constituents of the group and the way they conducted themselves. Although they came with their own jar of palm wine, father who was well informed beforehand about their visit wanted to make an impression. To show that he would never be caught unprepared, he bought a special jar of palm wine of his own. The august visitors were entertained in father's house on a four-course meal.

1. FIRST COURSE: Presentation of the Kolanut by Father: Father offered and broke kolanut with the august assembly. Kolanut, a very small seed from the kolanut tree was and still is used to accompany the pouring of the libation to the gods and the ancestors, when requesting their special blessings on all events that would take place on the given special day. It was always a time-consuming process. The Presenter of the kolanut asked the gods and the ancestors to replenish their pockets, and the partakers of the kolanut asked the gods and the ancestors to grant them good health, long life, peace and prosperity.

2. SECOND COURSE: Presentation of Oil-bean Salad: The oil-bean salad, a popular delicacy in Igbo culture, was made with oil beans served with garden eggs and melon cakes.

3. THIRD COURSE: Hot/Main Meal: Cassava Fufu and Ukazi soup served together: The ukazi soup served in our part of Igboland could differ from what one might be served in various other villages of Igboland.

4. FOURTH COURSE: Take-Away Foods: The visitors were to take away some of the foods to their home and share with their extended families. The Take-Away foods consisted of a large chunk of well-cooked meat smoked in an open fire in such a way as to retain its juices, as well as some additional oil-bean salad well wrapped in wide cocoyam leaves.

On Mother's return from Father's house she hinted her suspicion that the visit was not an ordinary one and her belief that it was for something special. Marriage proposal at that time was made to the family and not directly to the girl concerned. While this might appear odd to other cultures, that was our way of life and manner of doing things. Father had beforehand invited his close kin. He now sent for some invited elders of our village to participate in the conversations that followed. When they came, they were entertained. They joined the gathering in laughter and exchange of stabbing jokes that satirized and mimicked each other's village. I sent my younger sister as a spy and a listening post to eavesdrop into their conversation, for it was not proper for me to be seen at the site of their meeting. My sister, smart and sharp as a razor, did not only report what was said, she mimicked what was said, who said what, and how he said it. She ran back and forth from the venue of the meeting at father house to us at the maternal house, and so kept us abreast of all the goings-on. She had somehow managed to slip through mother's scrutiny and went to father's house unseen, what with mother herself so busy going to and from father's house. When Mother realized what my younger sister was doing, she was not in the least happy about her activities. One time, my sister came back and blurted out:

"Does he ever talk?"

"Does he ever talk? Who?" I retorted.

"Your husband, does he ever talk?"

"My husband!? I don't have a husband."

"Oh, yes, you do, or you will soon have one. He just sits there and listens to all they say, without opening his mouth."

"Why does he not say something? How do you know he hasn't said anything?"

Before I could finish my questions, my sister had dashed out again. When next she came back, she reported that father asked Amamba some direct questions about what he did for a living. She beamed with pride, because Amamba whom she was convinced was my husband and whom she said did not talk showed he could talk.

"And you know what? He is on a one-month leave from his work. He has finished his college education and lives and works in Port Harcourt. He says he saw you in the market and is determined to marry you."

Mother came in just as I was about to retort and commanded me to dress up and follow her to father's house where my presence was required. I had no room to question mother's authority. Father had said to come and I had to obey his command. Mother led the way and I followed her. By the time mother and I arrived at father's house, the party there had swelled to include father's other wives, who were drinking the palm wine offered to them. All eyes were on me when I walked into the room. The most exasperating part of the drama was that everyone was looking at me as though they were seeing me for the first time in their lives. Father's wives discerned me with pride and great amazement. Amamba contemplated me with appreciation and great relief. Father looked at me with pride and joy. The elders observed me with pride and a sense of protection. Mother, for her part, guided my every step with pride and a smile that could be interpreted in many different ways. Amamba's people looked on in awe. I felt like a fish out of the water in this group. I blurted out a greeting, which was lost instantly in the conversation that had resumed among all the people gathered there. I bowed my head and focused my attention on the floor. I was well aware that mother was watching my every move and I knew fully well that she would reprimand me later if any of my actions was improper. I wondered whether any of the things my sister reported was true. I hoped they were, for I was attracted to Amamba. The kind of desire coursing through my veins at that time was forbidden in our culture for a girl yet unmarried. My imagination ran wild. But, then, Father's voice brought me back to the present.

"Ọla, I called you to come and greet our guests."

That was a first time for me and a different gesture by my father. In the past, we had had visitors, but he never summoned me to greet them.

"Ọla, meet your own special visitors," he continued.

Amamba's mother came forward and embraced me warmly, referring to me as her friend and daughter. The other visitors in turn shook my hand, holding it and squeezing it for longer than was necessary. Amamba's handshake was different. He squeezed my hand and held it longer than all the other hand shakers put together. His eyes focused on me held an unspoken appeal, namely, to give a positive response to their marriage proposal when they tabled it. He was counting on me not to refuse him. Soon enough after, father dismissed me. I went back to our house, that is to say, our mother's house.

Long after the visitors left, mother returned to our house. My sister had brought us up to date before mother revealed to me the intentions of our special visitors. My parents, father's wives and the invited village elders had listened to Amamba's father ask for my hand in marriage to his son. My parents had thanked the visitors warmly and asked them to go home and allow them adequate time to ruminate on their proposition.

"But, I like the man, mother," I blurted out.

"Let me not hear you say that again, if you know what is good for you!" she hushed me up. "It is not proper for you to be too forward in a matter of this nature. Besides, even if you like him, you don't make it so apparent or people would have a poor assessment of your behavior."

"I don't care what people say. This is not like the time when you promised me in marriage to a man about whom I knew nothing, a man who was old enough to be my father. Don't you see that this man is well-educated, has a job and can take care of me?" I said.

"You do not live in this house with your Whiteman's education that has turned your head and made you disrespectful to our culture. I don't want people thinking that I have raised a man-crazy daughter. We all have to follow the tradition and that includes you," Mother said.

"You and the tradition, every day tradition," I said.

Mother had heard enough from me and was getting angry by the minute, even though in the past she had admired my boldness and outspokenness, which sometimes were too much for her.

"Listen, young girl, I don't want what they taught you in the school to become the rule in this house. When you are in my house, you have to abide by our tradition. And, right now, shut your mouth up and get my bath water ready."

That was it for the night. Mother had spoken her final word and I had heard it. Getting ready the water for her hot bath was usually my last assignment of the night. Mother liked her bath really hot, for she believed there was no better cure for aching bones and muscles than a really hot bath. I boiled the water in a large cast iron pot, which doubled as a bathtub. I hated taking a bath with mother, for I could not stand the temperature of the water. First, she would dip a native woven cloth into the hot water and dab it on all her joints, including her neck. Then, she would scrub her whole body with a special soap and sponge. Next, she rinsed off the soap with laps of water she scooped up with both palms cupped together. Lastly, she wrung the towel dry and dried her body with it. That method of taking bath conserved water; the streams were far away and it was difficult to fetch enough water for daily use in the compound.

On days when it was Mother's turn to sleep with father, she took extra care with her toiletries. She applied special ointment with a sweet-smelling fragrance on her body. I imagined father liked her that way, seen that the next day he gazed lovingly at her all day long. When one of us was ill, mother insisted on giving us the hot bath she believed was a panacea for all aliments. She exerted a lot of energy dabbing our joints and stretching our muscles. It worked magic towards our recovery, yet we dreaded it.

But to return to the prospective in-laws' visit: It had been three market weeks since Amamba, his parents and selected elders from their village paid a visit to my parents. My father sent word to them through Agu, the middleman. My parents, or should I say my father and the elders, had come to a deci-

sion about their marriage proposal and had a favorable answer for their offer. I was made to understand that their marriage proposal was acceptable. Mother shared my positive
feelings about their proposal with father. I gathered that the
day Amamba saw me in the market he came specifically to
look for a bride. Agu hailed from the same village as he and
accompanied him. He directed him to the market to see if I
was at the market that day with my mother. He had told him
beforehand that he knew a girl from a very good family.
Amamba came along not knowing what he would find. He
was pleased with what he saw, for he fell for me the moment
he laid his eyes on me. He went home and told his parents that
he had seen a girl he would want to marry. He was so convinced about his feelings that he gave them an ultimatum to
approve of his choice or he married some other girl from another town. His parents did not want their first son to marry
outside the town, for that would create a problem for their image and family tradition. They decided to pay a visit to my
parents.

Before their first visit, Amamba's parents conducted a
thorough investigation into my family through Agu, the middleman. The main intention of the investigation was to collect
all possible information about my family history, good and
bad, to avoid any embarrassing and unforeseen disclosures in
the future. They were very discreet in their investigation, yet
left no stone unturned to ascertain they were making the right
decision. They wanted only the best for their son, who was the
heir of the family. They did not interview any close relatives of
the bride-to-be. At the beginning of every interview session,
the interviewer exchanged pleasantries with the interviewee to
relax him or her. The interviewer covered four main areas:
Family History, The Mother, The Daughter, and The Father,
who was also the Head of the Family:

FAMILY HISTORY
  • What sort of family is it?

- Has there been a case of mental illness in the family?
  - Do the family members live long?
  - Do they die young?
  - Do they have adequate farmland?
- Has any family member been accused of or been caught stealing?
- Has any family member been accused of poisoning someone?
  - Are family members pure, honest and reliable?

THE MOTHER
- Is the mother a faithful and reliable wife?
- Has she ever committed adultery?
- Is she a hardworking woman?
- Has she ever been caught stealing?
- Is she a good cook and can she entertain guests?
- Is she a peaceful wife and mother?
- What is her relationship with other wives?
- Is she fertile?
- How well does she raise her children?
- Is she good to other wives, mothers and their children?

THE DAUGHTER
- Is she head-strong?
- Is she promiscuous?
- Is she respectful and obedient to her elders?
- Does she wander about too far from home and too often?
- Is she hard working, especially in the farm?
- Does she work closely with her mother?

THE FATHER, HEAD OF THE FAMILY
- Is he a spouse abuser?

- Is he fair to all wives?
- Does he manage the family well?
- Is he an avid farmer?
- How big is his barn?
- Does he drink excessively?
- How well does he feed his family and entertain his guests?
- Does he often borrow and owe money to others?

Evidently, Amamba's family was satisfied with their investigation, given their prompt decision to visit my parents and ask for my hand in marriage. My people, in their turn, investigated Amamba's family over a period of three weeks. They had to be thorough in their investigation, given that in marriage a woman was not equal to her husband. She was submissive to her husband and subordinate to him. They needed to ascertain up to a degree that their daughter would not be abused. Hence, they sought answers to the following questions and more: Family History, Amamba, Amamba's Mother, and Amamba's Father. My people believed in the adage, *Ihe nte muru aghaghi igho nte,* (what is begotten by a cricket cannot be anything else other than a cricket), meaning, *like father, like son* in English:

FAMILY HISTORY
o   How large is their family compound?
o   Does the family compound have adequate farmlands to feed all its members?
o   Has there been mental health disease in the family?
o   Do the family members live long?
o   Do family members die young?
o   Has any family member been accused of theft?
o   Has any family member been accused of poisoning someone?
o   Are family members pure, honest and reliable?

AMAMBA
- o What type of work does he do for a living?
- o How often does he visit home?
- o How caring is he towards his parents?
- o How well does he relate to his siblings?
- o How well does he relate with his kith and kin in the village?

AMAMBA'S MOTHER
- o What is her status in the family?
- o How many children has she given birth to in the family?
- o What is her character like?
- o Is she strong and resilient?
- o How well does she relate with other women in the family?
- o What is her reputation in the village like?
- o How able is she in farming and trading?

AMAMBA'S FATHER
- o Is he a wife abuser?
- o Is he fair and just to all wives and children in his compound?
- o How well does he manage his family?
- o Is he a great farmer and how big are his farmlands?
- o Is he a good provider for his family?

Mother had insisted on getting acceptable answers to these questions, for she did not want her daughter married into a family where spousal abuse was frequent and rampant, a family in which men easily got enraged and beat up their wives. Customarily, though, we believed a husband could reprimand and sometimes beat up a recalcitrant wife to maintain control and keep her in line. Mother was so convinced that she had trained me so well, especially to work hard, cook and clean, and show respect to elders, that I should have no problems in my marriage. Although Agụ, the middleman, had assured my parents that Amamba's parents were well-to-do, owned rich barns stacked with yams harvested from their large farms, mother insisted on knowing that her daughter would not starve:

"Luckily," she proudly explained her stance, "there are other suitors that want to marry my daughter, and I am only looking out for the best for her."

On the second visit of Amamba's people to our compound, Mother cooked even more food than she did for their first visit and made her best soup yet. They came with more jars of palm wine than the first time. Father, for his part, provided his own three jars of palm wine and two bottles of illicit gin. Amamba came with a bottle of Schnapps. This time around, he was allowed into mother's house to greet us. Actually, he wanted to see me before the upcoming long visit between my parents and his relatives. As usual, both sides took a lot of time stabbing each other with bad jokes, after which the kolanut was presented. The party consumed the fufu and soup and, going by the way they licked their fingers, testified the meal was delicious. Then, the serious matter of their visit was reintroduced for discussion. After a long period of deliberation, father assured them he was happy about their visit and offer, adding that he would be happy to establish an in-law relationship between the two families and their two villages.

Reader! Do not be fooled! Do not think by any stretch of imagination that parents made all the decisions for the bride-to-be in any marriage negotiation! On the face value it seemed so, but in reality it was not. Her consent was sought in the whole transaction before any commitments were made! *My* consent was sought in the whole process of my marriage. Thus far, observe that only the wine my father presented was consumed, not the wine the visitors brought. Their wine was not to be touched until I gave my consent for them to do so. Father

sent for me and told me of the intentions of visiting Amamba
and his family. He assured me that I was not under pressure to
do anything, adding that it was entirely up to me to indicate
my willingness to marry Amamba by drinking the first cup of
the wine they brought. Before all of this, mother had already
prepared me on how to behave in the presence of the visitors. I
was not to drink the whole cup of wine, but should take a sip
only to convince all present of my good manners. Drinking or
gulping up the whole cup of wine would not only be seen as
gluttonous, it would be in bad taste. When I received the cup
of wine, I focused my eyes on mother. She used body language to communicate to me what to do. I had no intention of
repeating any of my past mistakes in public. Mother did not
chastise me, but the look of disappointment on her face said it
all. Recalling now in my mind's eye that look of disappointment on her face, I dreaded the probable outcome back at her
house if I committed another gaffe that day.

When I received the cup of wine to drink, the buzzing
room fell utterly quiet and all eyes were fixed on me. There
and then, I realized the power I had in the whole transaction. I
was the key player. I looked at mother for cues, but for the first
time in our nonverbal communication none was forthcoming
from her. Father focused his attention somewhere else, away
from me. All the guests focused their eyes on me. Amamba's
eyes were especially pleading and anxious. It seemed to me
that I was on my own.

"What do I do now?" I asked myself. The power I felt I
had seemed to have dropped away.

Then, I decided to get it over and done with. Although I
had resolved to show all that I was an educated girl, I suc-
cumbed and acted as mother had instructed me to do, so as
not to disappoint her. I took the cup of palm wine, sipped
from it ever so daintily and handed it back to Father. Father
heaved a sigh of relief. Amamba heaved a sigh of relief, too.
The conversation resumed. Laughter erupted in the room.

"This is our daughter that we took good care to raise," the elders from my village proclaimed jubilantly.

The drinking resumed with each village claiming their own palm wine was better than the other's. Before Amamba and his people left that night to go home the date was set for the engagement ceremony.

Chapter 7

The Engagement

FOR THE ENGAGEMENT CEREMONY, THE *Ekwe-lam/Ekwebeghim* event, literally *I agree/I disagree*, which was the last ritual in the marriage transaction process, Agụ was still the selected middleman as he has been throughout the entire process of the marriage transaction. He was asked to advise and educate Amamba's parents on all the essential customary expectations from the would-be in-laws. Mother had to find out from other mothers whose daughters had been married before hers what gifts to expect from the in-laws for the mother, for other village women and for age mates of the girl to be married. The list was exhaustive. Among other items on the long list, the in-laws were expected to buy the following:

- o Wrapper for the mother
- o Pomade for the village women
- o Pomade for the girl's age mates
- o Bath soap for the mother
- o Bath soap for the age mates of the girl
- o Bath soap for the village women
- o Sweet-smelling talcum powder for the mother
- o Sweet-smelling talcum powder for the girl's age mates
- o Sweet-smelling talcum powder for the village women

Altogether, Amamba's family was required to provide 18 jars of pomade, 18 bars of bath soap and 18 tins of talcum powder for distribution to the women of the village. The womenfolk insisted on asking for even more gifts, saying that I was highly educated and considered to be one of their best daughters in the village. Additionally, they argued, I was a trainee in a teacher's training college at the time and would become a salaried worker after graduation. As such, the beneficiaries of my training would be Amamba and his village only, leaving my father and his village as losers and empty-handed. Indeed, the women of our village advised my mother to double the number of gifts demanded of the in-laws:

"She is the first daughter of her parents. She comes from a good compound. She has many suitors who may be willing to give more. If they want a cheap wife, they should look elsewhere," they argued.

"Our Ọla will reward them over and above what we are demanding," they chanted.

"The type of education our daughter is getting warrants reciprocity of some kind," they concluded.

On the day that the in-laws brought their traditional gifts, they were again entertained. But, something else happened. Mother refused the wrapper she was given, saying that it was of cheap quality. The village women complained that the size of their pomade jars was smaller than expected. They asked that they be taken back and replaced either with larger jars or more of the smaller ones to make up for the deficit. Observe that these complaints and requests were made over heated arguments between the in-laws. In not so many words, my people called Amamba's people stingy, accusing them of wanting to get a wife with the least amount of spending. Amidst the eating and drinking Amamba's people stabbed back my people, calling them greedy. An onlooker would have thought they would get into blows with one another, seen the way they were talking at the top of their voices. Eventually, the matter was settled. Amamba's father agreed to make up the deficit with money payment. The women present broke out in a joyful song of celebration, for they felt they had fought and won in the argument. They continued their drinking and feasting till late in the evening. The shouting and abusive language thrown from one side to the other that day, though playful, displeased me, to say the least. I was not so happy also, because Amamba was going to return to his station the following day. This event, *Ekwelam/Ekwebeghim*, was the last in a long process of marriage transaction that completed my engagement to Amamba. At the end of the long annual school vacation, I went back to complete my education as a trained teacher.

It became more and more evident that at the end of the school year I would graduate from the Teacher Training College and become eligible to work for the Mission schools. The fact did not sit well with my father, for he knew that teaching implied earning a salary, which could be used to train other children of his compound. He felt that the timing of my engagement was not beneficial to him. He aired his feelings later, during another event in the marriage process, asking that I be allowed to work for his family for at least a year. This opened up an opportunity for discussion in the correspondences between Amamba and me. He poured out all his emotions on the pages of his long letters to me, letters which were some eight pages long each time. I read and reread each of them several times. I slept with them under my pillow. I carried the latest in the crock of my brassiere. I always had a problem with writing long letters, partly because I did not know what to say and partly because mother's warnings inhibited all my activities. My inhibitions came from the fact that mother drummed into my head the role expected from a good daughter, which included not being forward and proactive in relationships with men. She trained me to be demure, unassuming and never to look at a man straight in the face.

"My daughter, never allow a man to see you looking directly in his face," she told me.

In every argument with my mother she won, she was the winner in every way.

My letters to Amamba told generally of events connected with my school work and my general health. There was no mention of being in love with him or missing him, even though I felt I loved him and missed him. But, come to think about it, how could one miss someone she had never touched or even to whom she had never sat close? However, I did have strong and compelling feelings and I thought I liked/loved him because he was handsome. His letters poured in weekly. Sometimes, I shared them with my friends, who again envied me and thought I was the lucky one. What was even more baffling to me was that marriages contracted in my time lasted till death did the married man and woman part. Marriages at that time seemed to me to be a big gamble, but they lasted more than those contracted with wooing, dating, and courting with roses and kisses. Marriages in those days were not merely contracts between a man and a woman, but rather between families, villages, and even communities. At the completion of a marriage in those days, the girl was referred to as *our* wife, and the families and villages referred to one another as *our* in-laws. They bailed one another out, when problems arose. The partaking in the kolanut, foods and drinks welded them together in a long-lasting union. They shared one another's joys and sorrows. They did not allow divorce or separation to tarnish the family image. The two families looked into every discord between the husband and wife. Long-lasting marriages were cultivated. Marriage bonds at that time could be likened to *the type of bond that held the three musketeers together.*

Once upon a time, a girl friend of mine got married. But, she got so homesick that she ran back to her village. Her father stood her at the compound gate and reprimanded her for tarnishing the family image. Her mother and her father's wives scolded her, calling her lazy and spoilt. The villagers showed her no mercy, for they too felt she was spoiling the good relationship between the two villages. She became more miserable in her maternal home than she was at her husband's place. After a few days and a lot of advice from her mother, father and stepmothers, her mother returned her to her husband's place with apologies on her behalf. For many years after that incident, she was referred to as the 'runaway wife'. Had she been welcomed back to her natal home and allowed to stay there for a long time, it would have been seen as a breach of tradition. Had she refused to return to her marital home, her parents would have been asked to pay back all the expenses made on her head. Marriage in my culture worked in those days, partly because culturally it was expected to be a lifetime commitment and partly because the girl was not allowed to question anything. She was a second-class citizen in the entire contract and was expected to live solely to please her husband. She addressed him with respect and never was on a first-name basis with him. He made all decisions of importance for her. It was only after many years of cohabitation with her husband and the mellowing of tradition from the passing of years that she was considered capable to make some major decisions about her life. Whichever way you chose to consider tradition-al marriage, the wife had to *stoop to conquer*, meaning, had to make a deliberate decision to lower her status as a wife and a human being, in order to gain recognition as a decision maker vis-à-vis her husband.

Amamba and his people continued to visit for days and months following the engagement. Their intention was to dis-courage other suitors and to mark me as taken. It was like tag-ging an article and putting it on lay-away, reserved exclusively for a particular buyer. On each festive occasion in the village, Amamba and his parents came bearing gifts of palm wine. They, in their turn, were also lavishly and sumptuously enter-tained with special meals to impress and remind them of the benefits that would accrue to them from the marriage. Some of us that were too young at the time to understand all the impli-cations of those visits saw them as opportunists exploiting the in-laws to get back a greater proportion of what they paid as bride price. They were always the first to arrive and the last to leave. Culturally, they were expected to participate in and partake of all the kolanut presented to other visitors. The annoying part of it all was that they were very loud and boastful, informing anybody that cared to listen that I was their wife. We watched all the drama unobserved and in silence. My siblings and I would bet to see whether or not they were indeed going to partake again in another meal served to other visitors. All the time, we were right. They would feign that they were merely going to taste the food, only in the end to join fully in the eating of the food. We concluded that they were at once ill-mannered, greedy and gluttonous. Boy, did we hate their visits! For each occasion, as soon as we saw them coming we would echo:

"Here they come again!"

How they so liked our family and my mother's cooking!

Mother reprimanded us each time we showed anger about their visits. She explained to us that their visits meant a lot in the in-law relationship they were in the process of forging, adding that their coming on occasions was their way of showing they cared. Indeed, each time they came, our glum facial expression showed our resentment of them as intruders. That was our young peoples' opinion. The adults knew better and received them with open arms.

Chapter 8

The Homecoming

THE MONTHS HAD FLOWN BY. I had finished my education at the Teachers Training College and had been working for almost a year as well. It was then that the in-laws indicated that it was time to arrange for my homecoming. Although my parents would have preferred that I worked a little longer to help my family, yet they acknowledged that the in-laws had been very patient.

Mother started very early to prepare for the homecoming of her first daughter, so that she would not be found wanting in any way. Homecoming in that sense meant that her daughter, her first daughter, would be leaving her maternal home for her husband's home. She knew well that her ability to entertain would be judged by all, so she consulted other mothers that had passed through the same kind of experience before her to learn firsthand how to proceed. She combed all the nearby village markets, taking note of where things were sold and where to purchase things she needed at a good price. She pursued special bargains and got the best possible deals for her money's worth. She was a prolific farmer, but bought food items that she did not cultivate in her farm. She had also bought homemaking items, which she intended to give me as departing gifts. Those items would be shown publicly and would constitute a means of measuring her worth. Besides, that was her first experience of such a special event, not to mention that it was her first daughter that was about to get married. She, therefore, had a double task of making good of the homecoming. Her prestige in the village depended on it. People will judge her on how she did it, what she did, and the number and quality of the items she bought for the departing ceremony of her first daughter. The older village women and mothers, whose daughters had been married before me jointly made the assessment of the bridal trousseau as either adequate or inadequate. Traditionally, the family must provide some basic homemaking items for the young bride-to-be:

✓ Tripods for holding cooking pots above the fire
✓ Cooking pots of various sizes and shapes
✓ Mortar and pestle for processing and grinding all ingredients needed for cooking
✓ Wooden spoons of various sizes for cooking
✓ Large clay pots for fetching and storing water
✓ A live hen to ensure and enhance the fertility of the bride

Whichever way the assessment of the bride's trousseau went--sufficient and satisfactory or insufficient and unsatisfactory--it made a clear statement that confirmed the family image as good and boosted it or shamed it as bad and lowered it. The family prestige, therefore, hung precariously on the departing presents given to the bride-to-be and would constitute a topic of conversation among the villagers for many days after as women discussed and compared and contrasted what other families had given their own daughters for their homecoming. Moreover, the assessment of the trousseau also served to differentiate the village haves from the have-nots and judged a family according to its shortcomings. No family wanted to be found wanting. The zeal for competition among the families was such that every family strove to outdo the others.

Traditional expectations varied widely and were different even among people who spoke the same Igbo language but different dialects. In modern times, however, these practices

have significantly changed, for modernity has eroded traditional culture over time. Nowadays, home going items include
such expensive items as refrigerators, cars and electronic home
appliances. The criteria for assessment of the bridal departing
presents have also changed. Modern men now opt to marry
wives that would enhance their status rather than those that
would constitute liabilities for them.

But to return to the homecoming event: Time was of the
essence for mother. At a time when food processing was manually done from scratch, she felt she had a lot to do to prepare
for my homecoming. Mother sent my siblings and me several
times during the market weeks to fetch firewood for cooking
our daily meals. Some of the firewood would also be saved for
the preparation of the big meals on my homecoming day. We
did not go alone to fetch firewood, my siblings and I. No. Other children volunteered to go with us, knowing fully well that
mother would remunerate them well on the big day. The more
the number of children participating meant more firewood
fetched and the merrier and safer the company was for everyone. We stored most of the firewood fetched in the backyard of
mother's house. Mother also assigned to us the task of shelling
the unshelled melon seeds she bought from the market. It was
an arduous and time-consuming task that we could not have
possibly accomplished alone. More hands were still needed for
the onerous task of shelling the melon seeds and so Father's
other wives and mother's relatives got involved. We sent out
oral invitations for help and people responded, including
those that were invited and others that were not invited. There
were some people whose presence we frowned upon, but we
welcomed them all the same. Absence of Friends and loved
ones on such occasions was interpreted as hatred and mean-
ness on their part. Friends and relatives swarmed our compound daily to help in various tasks before the big day and
mother welcomed and entertained them as they came. Daily
as the need arose, parties went to the stream to fetch and store
water in earthenware pots for cooking and cleaning.

All the walls of the houses in our compound were painted with red mud. In addition, designs were made on them with black charcoal and white chalk. Everywhere looked clean and beautiful. They made a statement of their own. Some foods, like the melon cakes, were cooked ahead of time to ensure their firmness and readiness for the upcoming occasion. Then, they were dried in open embers to improve their taste and to preserve them. Among the entire layout of preparations, pounding the shelled melon seeds was a very tedious job. Often, able-bodied youths of the village were solicited to help, for the pounding of shelled melon seeds was best handled by adults. It took several hours of pounding to achieve the right consistency. Only experienced adults could tell the right amounts of the ingredients needed for the melon cakes. Even then, it was often a matter of trial and error. Echoes of the pounding of melon seeds rang out throughout the village. It was a welcome sound, for the people saw it as an eloquent sign that said they had done well by their daughter.

Owing to the unavailability of refrigeration at the time, meat needed for the soups was the last item bought the morning of the homecoming event. A large portion of the meat was cooked and dried in open embers that were still glowing after all the cooking was done. This large portion of meat was reserved and would become part of the in-laws' take-away food when they departed, food to be shared with their friends as testimony of how well they were received and entertained. The size of the traditional meat portion for this ritual must meet the expectations of my village elders. Where the meat portion failed to meet their approval, more meat would have to be added. The facial expressions of the in-laws mirrored their satisfaction or dissatisfaction. Activities related to the marriage ceremony of the bride and her home going to her husband's village could only be understood by the orchestration emanating from the various noises of ingredients being pounded in mortars, the laughter, shouts of greetings and friendly bantering among the in-laws. It was all a welcome noise, which ushered people from another village into the lives of their in-laws' village. Children and elders came to observe and participate in the occasion and were glad to partake of a free meal.

On the day of the event, the groom arrived with many of his friends anxious to witness firsthand the entertainment of the day, as well as meet the bride and partake of the feast. They also added to the crowd and joyful noise. Mother prepared a special pot of soup enriched with the best of all the ingredients, exclusively for Amamba's father and the elders from his village that accompanied him. First, they dug their fingers into the pot of the soup to ascertain that the contents measured up to their expectations. In the pot of soup were a large dried catfish, chunks of stock fish, bush meat, beef, snails and bails of melon cakes. Each of the many ingredients seemed to struggle for space in the soup, and made it impossible for their fingers to get to the bottom of the pot. As they worked their fingers through the soup, they nodded their heads with satisfaction. Then, they planned on how best to convey home the soup, which eventually they would show to the elders of the village the next day. Yes, Amamba and his father had good reason to brag to friends and foes about the good catch they had made in the marriage of their son. Uninvited friends outnumbered the groom's friends invited to the occasion.

The large number of the uninvited rendered a well-planned seating arrangement difficult to handle. Given that canopies were not available at the time, palm fronds were cut and erected to provide shelter from the sun and seats placed under the shelter for the people to sit. Father was well prepared for this great occasion. He went as far as to consult the best and the most reliable of the rain doctors, one that most people believed could make rain fall as well as prevent it from falling, in order to ensure that no rain fell to disrupt the ceremony. Many people believed in the particular rain doctor father retained. They saw him as an ally on such a special day as the homecoming. People relied on his magic, for quite often he was right in his claims. His charges were therefore higher than those of the lesser known rain makers. On occasions when his magic failed, he attributed the failure to the evil deeds of his competitors jealous that they were not consulted to check the rains. However, all that mattered on the day of a special event was that it did not rain. Therefore, we held his claims in awe. The Very Important Persons (V.I.P.s) of the occasion, who were mainly the elders of Amamba's village and those of our village, were seated in Father's house. Other important personalities were seated in Father's *Obu*, a special outhouse meant mainly for male elders. The elders were the keen decision makers of the village and each tried to protect the interest of their village. Many others were seated outside under the improvised palm fronds shelters. The visitors and hosts alike bantered all night, eating and drinking anything and everything that came their way.

Some people from the village sat at a far distance from the venue of the main activities. From their location they watched keenly the goings-on, making necessary and unnecessary demands of the in-laws. A list of acceptable requisitions from the in-laws had been passed down from past generations. Still, sometimes, it was not uncommon for the bride's people to inflate the numbers and quantities of the items on the list, in order to get more from the in-laws. Married women, uncles and bride's peers despite being fully in support of her marriage demanded gifts from the in-laws. They themselves gave mainly monetary gifts to the bride to support her in her married life. The popularity of a girl was measured by the amount of money she received at an event such as her home going ceremony. Good girls received a lot of gifts, whereas bad girls received less. The bride-to-be took all her monetary gifts to her marital home. How much control a husband would exert on his wife could be deduced from the way he handled those donations his wife received. A controlling husband would demand and take away all the money from her, whereas a loving husband would let her keep her money. Of course, there was a catch in that, too. Although a loving husband let his wife keep all her money, yet he expected her to include him in the spending of the money. A wise wife would always consult her husband, when she used the money and when there was need for her to spend her money. Hence, building trust into the foundation of the marriage invariably started with the wise use the wife made of her money. In the case of Ọla, the marriage started well. Amamba was so over the hill in love with her that he allowed her leverage in the use of her money. Besides, both of them were well-educated and so could afford to deviate a little from the strict traditional customs governing the use of the wife's money. Ọla's marriage had begun on a good note. The rest depended on her ability to build a good relationship with her parents-in-law, especially her mother-in-law.

Everything went according to plan on Ọla's homecoming day. There was no rain and so the rain doctor took credit by popular vote for a job well done. The numerous guests were satiated with food, palm wine, Whiteman's gin and other forms of entertainment. Father was so happy about the successful outcome of the whole event that he reverted to his Whiteman's manners, including speaking to people in Pidgin English. Mother could not contain herself. All her hard work of the past several weeks had paid off successfully in high dividends. Village women showered her with praises. They composed lyrics of impromptu praise songs with her name. Her name echoed in the village over and over again. Every member of our compound shared in the praises and credits of the day. Then, suddenly, like every good thing always did, the events of the day came to an end.

Before the start of the homecoming event Amamba put a plan in place that expedited the day's events, so that the activities did not drag on unnecessarily far into the night. He was determined to take his bride home, before dawn, and have a wink before the villagers started streaming into the compound to see the new bride. Consequently, he settled all of the customary expenses with his in-laws. He went to and from their homes to ensure that all the monies due to them were paid, and that no stones were left unturned. He hired a pickup van, a 'kit car," to convey the youths back and forth from his village to the in-laws' village. That was quite impressive, given the time period in question. The youths carried the palm wine required for the occasion. Amamba was in a mad haste to fulfill the motivation for all the marriage transactions that had taken place over the years. He dreamed of bringing home his bride, romancing her and having sexual intercourse with her. After all, the ulterior motive of all the arrangements he made was to consummate the union with his bride. However, he was disappointed, for whereas he was in a hurry his people preferred to linger, casually so, too. The unnecessary delay afforded them every opportunity they craved to consume more food and drinks. Then, again, the bantering among the in-laws lasted far into the night, further creating problems for Amamba. The first cock's crow that ushered in another new day shocked them, for only then did they realize just how far gone the night was. The cock's crow was a signal for the in-laws to hand over the bride to their in-laws and head home. Mother took me inside and prepped me up to look beautiful before handing me over to father, who would have the honor of handing me over to the in-laws. Father did not hand me over directly to the in-laws. No. He handed me over to his own father, who was the oldest elder in the compound. Grandfather then handed me over to Amamba's father.

"Igwe," said my grandfather. "This is my daughter whom we have raised up to be obedient, respectful and well-mannered. We are giving her over to you, because of the love and very deep respect we have for your family. As you can see, she is wholesome. She has no scars. If peradventure she misbehaves in such a manner that you no longer deem her fit for your family, please bring her back to us as whole as you are taking her away from our family to your family. On our part, we would not like to see her maltreated, abused, maimed, or neglected. Treat her as if she was your own daughter. We have trained her to respect you, serve you and learn to love you. She is all yours now."

At the conclusion of the ceremonies I left for Ajala, Amamba's village. Amamba and I were seated in the front seats of the pickup van. We arrived at Ajala very early in the morning. Amamba, the perfect gentleman, allowed me a few hours of uninterrupted sleep, while he waited patiently for the following night to consummate the marriage.

Our marriage, Amamba and Qla's, was not spiced with the well-known cliché *"What God has joined together, let no man put asunder."* No. What the marriage had was the blessings of the elders of two families and two villages that believed the marriage union had an everlasting bond that could not be broken by the couple on their own without the knowledge, consent and intervention of the other parties of interest involved. Indeed, in the past, marriages in our culture were very difficult to dissolve without incurring the wrath of parents, families, elders, villages and middlemen. Two villages did their best to make marriages between their children work. Moreover, the middlemen had a stake, for in each case they were handsomely remunerated for their roles towards ensuring the success of the marriage negotiations. Therefore, they put in every effort to see that the marriages worked, because they were judged by their successes in their prior engagements. Moreover, their future chances of being sought out to act as middlemen again in other marriages depended on their reputation. The two villages also played their part to see marriages last, due to the lasting trust and friendship established in a marriage by two villages. Hence, marriages were protected from all sides. No one wished to see a marriage break up, except in very serious offences like stealing, adultery and excessive quarreling. The adage and oath *for better or for worse* applied mostly to women, though. They must obey every wish of their husbands' families and live to make their husbands happy at all times. The scale always titled towards the wife, who must obey her husband and family and even give her consent when her husband wished to marry another wife to make himself famous and happy. The husband must marry another wife, if his wife was considered infertile and/or bore only female offspring. Hers was the heavier burden to bear compared to her husband's.

It was about sun set in Ajala village. The activities going on all day in Igwe's compound replaced all the expectations and the energetic anxiety of the past several weeks now over. Friends, relatives and visitors came in droves to be entertained and to see the face of the new bride. Igwe's joy knew no bounds. He had done it! He had brought home a wife for his son! What a prestigious achievement, for that matter! It meant that he could look forward to grandchildren that would sit on his aching laps in his old age! The visitors came to have a glimpse of the new bride and assess her beauty, manners and suitability for their favored and well-educated son, the pride of their village. They also were there to see what foods she brought home from her mother and partake of some of them. The heap of oil-bean salad and the number of melon cakes that came with it were enough and met their expectations. They could tell that their serving portions would be sizable. They salivated at the sight of full pots of palm wine yet untouched. Yes, indeed, Amamba had made a good choice. That was their verdict. How could they not be satiated with the abundance in food that Ọla's mother sent home with her? The take-away food she sent home with her in-laws surpassed all set standards. To the fifty balls of melon cakes required she had added forty more! The soup had more ingredients in it than was normally expected. And, of course, the mound of cassava fufu was high to the roof top, perhaps higher than the one Chinua Achebe so eloquently described in hyperbolic terms during an in-laws' get-together in his famous premier novel, *Things Fall Part*. Igwe, ordinarily difficult to satisfy, showered praises on his son, boasting that he searched well and found a befitting wife, not to mention worthy in-laws. Throughout the whole day, he raved about his good fortune, good in-laws, and the expectation of grandchildren in the near future, preferably grandsons, the first of whom would arrive in nine months. In his mind's eye, he pictured himself holding his grandson on his lap and the child pulling on his grey beard. To him, when it did happen, it would be another first in his life, yes, and a fulfillment of his life's dreams.

The following morning, again, Ọla, the new bride that had had very little sleep the previous night, kept busy entertaining the numerous visitors that came to the compound. And this went on the whole day. She kept a constant smile on her face, partly because her mother had tutored her to do so and partly because she was told that a smile enhanced her beauty and charm. Her set of white teeth, the glow of her brown eyes and the luster of her skin added to her natural beauty. Physically, she was pleasantly chubby, which body type was preferred by men at that time. They did not like skinny brides, for they claimed that they could not carry pregnancies to full term. A skinny body, they said, was a sign of health hazard. With our constant hot weather and no means of good preservation, all food brought home the previous night had to be dispensed with quickly. Especially the oil-bean salad that continued to ferment and would easily go bad had to be quickly consumed, though its deterioration would not have deterred the visitors from devouring it. The early birds had the best part of the foods. The late comers had the more fermented version of the salad that sometimes caused stomach aches and gas. But, did they care? No. The melon cakes kept better than the oil-bean salad, because they were prepared by drying them over embers of fire. The two items of food, the melon cakes and the oil-bean salad, always went together. No matter what time the guests arrived, they requested that their own portions of the items were served together. Hence, only good management in distributing those items made them last longer than they normally would. The palm wine was used to wash down the food served. It continued to ferment, invariably became highly intoxicating, and made some guests more talkative into the bargain. All in all, everyone cherished and consumed the foods and was proud and happy. They described the new bride, Ọla, as the 'shining silver' her name portrayed her to be. She was nimble when she moved and when she smiled her face lit up and sprayed sunshine through her well-set teeth.

"Mmm, Mmm, is she beautiful!" the people exclaimed.

Nonetheless, Ọla had a multifaceted problem that day. To begin with, she was shy, for she was taught growing up that if she did not show shyness she would be branded presumptuous. Then, she was also feeling very tired from lack of sleep and weary from participating in the many events jammed into the last twenty-four hours, not to talk of the days before. Next, she was anxious into the bargain, for her mind was focused on the event that would inevitably take place that night. She was afraid of the event that loomed for the night. Her fears were based on misinformation that some indiscreet adults had given her when they talked to her about the excruciating pain to anticipate at the consummation of the marriage. Most of the pieces of false information she received were focused on the pain, rather than on the ecstasy that she had read about in some foreign books on love and romance.

Finally, it was sunset. The chickens had retired for the night and the many visitors in the compound had also gone away. Ọla's anxiety mounted. Constant, however, was Amamba's titillation. Pride and happiness were radiating in and through him. The previous day that the bridal homecoming dragged on Ọla had some relief. But, today, she must face the music. Amamba, for his part, was in frenzy and employed all tactics he could muster to bid the visitors goodbye. Some understood and took the hint. But others, especially his age mates, purposely delayed their departure to frustrate him. He took all in good stride, because all their taunting was in their right. It was their way of testing his patience. Eventually, they all left. By then, the village was engulfed in pitch darkness. All pounding in the mortar with pestles had ceased. It was an indication that supper had been eaten and it was time to go to

bed. Ọla was busy helping her mother-in-law prepare and
serve the evening meal. Supper over, she took a warm bath
and applied a sweet-smelling ointment that her mother had
given her for the consummation of the marriage. She had to
smell nice for her husband, her mother had told her.

What went on behind the closed bedroom doors that night
was better imagined than described. Amamba was radiating
happiness the next morning with everything he did. Ah! I understood why my mother-in-law took me in her arms and
showered me with words of endearment and wishes that a
grandchild would be hers in the following nine months. It was
a wish that was more often fulfilled than never fulfilled in our
culture, because the field of nurturing the wish was fertile and
there had been no tampering with it. My parents, especially
my mother, were informed of my virtue. Mother received ac-
colades for preserving my virginity for my husband, thus up-
holding the good image of the family. She received the gift of a
new wrapper, which she showed off to the women of our village. Looking back now to those days, it seems like a fairy tale.
Modern ethics, values and practices cannot understand it, for
playing the field is now permitted and acceptable.

All in all, Ọla had a good beginning in her marriage and in
her new village. Amamba was still very much in love with her
and gave her all freedom to excel in her new home. What was
left for her to do was to establish a good relationship with her
mother-in-law, with whom she would live for the first years of
her married life. Dutiful mothers, whose daughters were about
to be married, schooled them thoroughly on how to relate
with their in-laws. Total obedience ranked highest on the scale
of expectations and was seen as a window through which a
wife gained admission into her new family. She learned that a
new wife should never be in a hurry to establish her own
kitchen and that she had to stay with her mother-in-law to
learn all she could about the new family, taking note of the
foods they enjoyed and how best to prepare them. She was not
to take care of her husband only, but must also consider the

responsibility of taking care of her father-in-law. She needed to care for his needs regularly, just as she did with her own father. Good marks earned in forging all these relationships would enhance her overall assessment and result in her protection should problems arise in her marriage. The list of mothers' teachings to their daughters before marriage was endless, especially given that mothers always had it in the back of their minds that they too were constantly being judged along with their daughters. Hard work was expected of every wife, new or old. No husband wanted to be burdened with a lazy wife that slept in most mornings.

Ọla's husband had many siblings. Some of them were older and some younger than Ọla. Still some were the same age as she. Those of her age competed with her, daring her to outperform them in some activities. Sometimes, they left most of the tasks for her to accomplish. They would want her to prove that she could fetch more firewood than them or carry bigger pots for fetching water. These competitions were nothing to Ọla, because she had gone through them before in her village and had proven that she was the strongest of all her mates. In singing and dancing she surpassed them all and invariably most of them made friends with her, so that she could teach them her dance steps. They admired her, because she was friendly disposed towards them and very willing to teach them what she knew. On the other hand, the older siblings of her husband sometimes wanted her to serve them, just to find faults with her. Ọla struggled to do all she could to accommodate those many demands on her in her marriage. Her mother-in-law, who loved her very much, intervened to mitigate the demands on her. She set up a routine for all concerned to follow, so that Ọla's work was not too much for her. Her father-in-law was too busy running the whole compound to be bothered about such trivial matters, although all serious matters were invariably brought to his attention. In the morning, Ọla must wake up early. Ọla must sweep the rooms of their house. Ọla must join in sweeping the compound. Ọla must rush to the stream to fetch water. Ọla must ensure that food was prepared. Ọla must serve food to her husband. Ọla must be seen as up and doing. Ọla must wear a smile on her face as she worked, for a sour face would be interpreted as unwillingness on her part to work. That was how the journey that started with two people, two villages and two families came to a successful new life.

Chapter 9

The Marriage

ỌLA WAS HAPPY IN IGWE'S compound. She was wholly accepted there by its members and the villagers. The relationship between the in-laws grew strong to such an extent that their confidence in one another flourished. Their visits to one another did not lessen, rather they increased. The parents of the new wife were equally invited to visit their in-laws on special occasions. They exchanged presents freely and mutually. Gift giving was no longer a one-way traffic. Amamba loved me so much that he was very willing to do anything that would make me happy. His peers thought that I had put a charm on him. Others said that I had given him a love potion to make him love me the way he did. My days were joyous. I discharged with ease many activities that went with marriage, which no longer constituted hard work for me. My mother-in-law continued to shower praises on me. She had me under her wings and I felt secure and at home as if I was still in my maternal home. Of course, Amamba and I moved to his station, where I easily obtained a teaching job. My salary went into our common savings account and we decided together what we did and how we helped our two families. Thus, my parents' fear of losing their educated daughter's constant support disappeared. This is because we helped them in raising their many children, meaning, all the children in the extended family, including my half-siblings. Mother did not resent this spreading of wealth to the extended family; I made sure that she lacked nothing and had no reason to be jealous of anyone. The sequence of all these events justified the early belief people held about me dating back especially to when I was an infant bride, to the effect that I was a girl born into luck.

"She is lucky!" they said. Truly, I felt I was not only just lucky but also blessed in every way.

There remained yet another expectation from the bride, which I must fulfill for the marriage union to be complete; conception, the main reason for the marriage in the first place, especially for the parents of my husband. Not only did my parents-in-law await the news of my conception, my parents equally did. With anxious expectation Mother inquired from people in my village whether they had seen me recently, and if there were any noticeable changes on my body to indicate that I was pregnant. Three months after my homecoming and no signs of pregnancy mother began to panic, thinking that the waiting period was going to be protracted as it was in her own case. For some unknown reason, I did not get pregnant as soon as expected. But, when news of my first pregnancy broke, mother was overjoyed. She proclaimed that once again God had vindicated her. I did not quite know what the hurry for me to get pregnant was all about. All I was aware of was that certain changes were taking place in my life. Morning sickness attacked me. I had no knowledge about that before then and it disrupted some of my daily activities. When my mother and my mother-in-law heard of my predicament, they bombarded me with many spices and other food items deemed to be palliative remedies for my condition. Each mother was eager to make the train journey to our station to help me out. But Amamba dissuaded them from coming, adding that everything was under control. Waiting for the miracle to happen took nine long months. But, happen it did, eventually. At the end of the gestational period a baby girl was born into Igwe's family. My mother-in-law was so overjoyed at the news that she summoned Ajala village women to accompany her to my maternal village to inform their in-laws. That was not just a simple visit. It only sounded so. There was no forewarning. Unprepared as Mother was for their visit, she still had to entertain them as though their visit had been planned. Their jubilation, drum and gong beats heralded their coming and alerted mother, who had been waiting over the months to hear the good news. Father released yams from his barn for their entertainment, which began in earnest with women from my maternal village joining in the birth song and dance. The longer they stayed, the more food and drinks they were served and the more passers-by came into the compound to see what was going on and join in the eating and merriment.

News of a granddaughter was welcomed, but my father-in-law wanted more, a grandson. Thus, another expectation loomed in Ọla's life. She was subtly reminded that more was expected of her, a son. At that time, long periods of breastfeeding and abstinence were employed for family planning. However, my father-in-law was not going to brook those as reasons enough not to produce a son and grandson in his family. He kept asking whether there was any new news from my new family that had escaped his eagle eyes. Amamba always came to my rescue, but could not quite stop his anxiety. Two years after the birth of our first daughter, I became pregnant and passed through the ordeal of morning sickness all over again. This time around, however, I had learned from my first experience and carried the pregnancy better than the first time. When the good news reached all expecting with me over the months that I had delivered a second child, this time a son, the joy and celebrations went on for days on end. *For unto Igwe's compound a son was born, one that would carry the family name! Mission accomplished!* Amamba, equally elated, overjoyed and barely able to control himself, carried the news to his parents. He proudly went to my village to announce the news in person. Igwe, his father, made a special trip to see my father. They congratulated each other for their good fortune, which consolidated their relationship and friendship and also made them feel that they had a lot in common. They set aside a special day for the naming ceremony of our son, just as it was done for our daughter. Friends were invited from other towns and villages and the entertainment went far and beyond the two villages.

So began another Igwe generation in Ajala village. And the love between Amamba and Ọla prospered over the years.